"One o'clock. There's a MiG-28 headed straight for us."

The news didn't worry Zach. Since the Gulf War, Iraqi and American fighters did everything they could to avoid confrontation.

"He's not supposed to be in the no-fly zone. Let's chase him home," he ordered, putting his jet into a quick U-turn that would bring him in low on the bogey.

"Copy. Got you covered, Tomcat Leader." Michelle then followed his lead.

The MiG pilot had enough maneuvers to keep them on the edge of their seats as they raced through the skies at speeds that exceeded the sound barrier. Something wasn't right. Zach felt it in his gut.

If this was all for laughs, the MiG pilot would have bugged out by now. This guy was playing cat and mouse as if he wanted to get caught. Which could mean only one thing—*he* was the cheese. So they'd better keep their eyes open....

"Two more bogeys closing in, Zach."

The dogfighting was fast and furious after that, with three MiGs and two Tomcats vying for supremacy.

"He's got a lock." Michelle put her Tomcat into a barrel roll, launching chaff to confuse any heat-seeking missiles. "I can't shake him."

Then it happened. The MiG fired, scoring a direct hit. The tail of Michelle's Tomcat burst into flames. Her plane spiraled toward the ground.

Sign, SEAL, Deliver
Rogenna Brewer

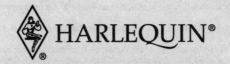

HARLEQUIN®

TORONTO • NEW YORK • LONDON
AMSTERDAM • PARIS • SYDNEY • HAMBURG
STOCKHOLM • ATHENS • TOKYO • MILAN • MADRID
PRAGUE • WARSAW • BUDAPEST • AUCKLAND

ISBN 0-373-70980-3

SIGN, SEAL, DELIVER

Dear Reader,

My father was an Air Force veteran, and after he left the service he obtained a private pilot's license. He and my mother honeymooned in Niagara Falls and he caught a 7.25-pound walleye there. The fish was mounted and stuffed and in my possession until it simply disintegrated years later. That's pretty much all I know about my father, because he died in an auto accident at the age of twenty-six—six months before I was born.

My mother's parents were very much a part of my life as I was growing up. And most of the stories I know about my father were told to me by my grandma. One such tale was how she'd run outside the house on Bank Street in Fond du Lac, Wisconsin, waving a dishcloth, every time she heard a plane overhead—just in case it was my dad. Grandma once told me her only regret was that she'd never flown with my father.

Grandma died of cancer when I was a young mother with two sons, and I mourned her daily. About a year after she died, during a rare afternoon nap, I found myself in a state of twilight sleep with tears spilling from my eyes. I heard Grandma's voice as clearly as if she were in the room. "Don't cry, Genna, I'm flying with your dad now."

My tears dried that day because I had not one but two guardian angels. I have a lot of fond memories of my grandma. I have only memorabilia from my dad: the flag that draped his coffin, his name—given to me by my mother when I was born—the ring he gave my mother on their wedding day, and his pilot's wings, which inspired me when I started to write this book.

Though I never knew him, I have felt my father's absence every day. I hope you enjoy the story I wrote for him and my grandmother.

Sincerely,

Rogenna Brewer

P.S. I'd love to hear from you. Write to me at Rogenna@aol.com

For the people missing from my life:

**My father, Roger William Bean
1934–1960**

**My grandmother, Grace Agnas Reschke Amend
1910–1987**

CHAPTER ONE

IN THIS PART of the ship a man alone risked a brush with nature, but Lieutenant Zach Prince didn't mind the tight squeeze through a passageway full of female personnel. Or the swat one junior officer delivered to his behind.

"Hey, hotshot, what's your hurry?"

Zach cocked a grin and carried on. "You ladies have been at sea too long." One hundred and sixteen days too long to be exact. Whatever the reason, at twenty-nine he rather liked the celebrity that came with being a Top Gun, the top one percent of naval aviators.

Tart language and feminine laughter followed his progress past cramped quarters shared by six female ensigns, a "six chick" in ship slang. The term smacked of sexism, but wasn't crude, compared to the idiom used for six male ensigns.

Zach sidestepped another whack. After all, he didn't want the produce bruised before it left the market. Patting the upper left pocket of his flight suit, the one closest to his heart, he started to whistle. And if it sounded a little like "Here comes the bride," well, that was probably because he was a man with a mission.

It had taken him the entire cruise, four months of having his advances shot down by a certain admiral's daughter, to finally figure it out. Women didn't want words that amounted to empty promises. Or even romance. They wanted commitment.

So even though he could feel a trickle of sweat running down the back of his neck toward the yellow streak that served as his spine, he was going to take the plunge and ask Michelle to marry him.

Reaching her stateroom, Zach delivered a preemptive knock and at the same time swung the hatch inward on its hinges. Stepping over the lip, he caught Michelle's roommate, Skeeter, in the middle of tugging on a T-shirt.

"Sorry," he said in apology.

"Don't you ever knock?"

"I knocked." He turned up the wattage on his smile, showing off even white teeth that had never needed braces. He'd learned to use that smile to his advantage at a very early age and managed to coax one out of her, as well, albeit a skeptical smirk.

"After the fact doesn't count, Prince."

Shrugging into her flight suit, she did a quick zip-up. The leather wings stitched to her uniform identified her as S. Daniels. He'd be damned if he could remember what the "S" really stood for; everyone just called her Skeeter. The navigator was Michelle's RIO, radar-intercept officer.

"Where's Her Royal Highness?"

Skeeter nodded toward the adjoining bathroom, and he rewarded the petite brunette with a quick kiss. She let out an exaggerated huff of annoyance.

"You know you love me, Skeeter."

"Keep dreaming, jet jock." She slammed her wardrobe shut and headed for the hatch, where she paused for effect. "If you get caught, it's not just your ass in a sling. It's hers, too."

After the RIO left, Zach stared long and hard at the closed portal. Deep down he knew Skeeter spoke the truth. But he chose to dismiss the warning. As far as he was concerned, his objective outweighed the risk. Rules were made to be broken. Or at the very least bent.

Besides which, Skeeter tended to be a bit overprotective when it came to her driver. Although the last person who needed someone looking out for her was Lieutenant Michelle Dann.

He heard the shower running even before he opened the door to the compact head. "Man on deck." He announced his presence, sweeping aside the white utility shower curtain.

Startled brown eyes that set off lovely rounded features met his. Everything about Michelle was rounded…and soft…

"Zach Prince! Don't you ever knock?"

…except her demeanor.

He winced. He hated it when she said his name as if it were a curse. "I already had this conversation with your roommate."

"Then maybe you should listen. For a change."

His wandering gaze traversed the slope of her dripping backside. Almost.

"Give me that." She snatched the shower curtain from him and used it for cover.

He'd long since etched every nuance of her body into his heart. "All you need, sweetheart, is that JP-5 you're wearing." JP-5—jet fuel—mingled with wash water on board. Sailors and aviators alike never really got rid of the smell during a cruise. They just got used to it.

On Michelle it was like the finest French perfume to his fighter pilot's soul. He breathed in its addictive scent.

"Get out." She tossed her head, whipping wet hair across the swell of her breasts.

Zach ignored the seriousness in her tone and reached out to finger a burnished-brunette strand. Just touching her ignited his desire...or looking at her...or thinking of her. ''Is there room in there for two?'' He knew from experience the stall barely held one. But he liked to imagine the possibilities.

''You know you're not supposed to be here, Zach. I could have you put on report.''

''So why don't you?'' he dared, knowing an empty threat when he heard one.

She heaved a frustrated sigh, finally admitting it to herself. ''You're going to get us both in trouble. You know that, don't you?''

''Only if we get caught.''

''My point exactly. It's only a matter of time. The Navy's cracking down on fraternization. You read the new policy, or knowing you maybe you haven't. But if you think I'm going to throw away my career just to be another hash mark on the helmet of some hotshot jet jock, you're sadly mistaken, mister.''

Zach didn't deny the statement. Like many other fliers, he had kills stenciled on his helmet and painted on his plane. He had four, one for every enemy fighter he'd shot down. Five would make him an ace.

Some guys put stickers on their helmets to mark

their conquests with women. Hash marks on Zach's helmet represented every time she'd shot him down, figuratively, not literally.

So far he'd suffered seventeen hits to his ego.

But this time would be different.

She was softening. He stared at her mouth as the tip of her tongue darted out to wet her full lips.

"You're not even listening to me, are you." Her brown eyes blazed from behind spiked lashes. "I absolutely hate that about you."

"I love it when you're riled." He'd listen when she said something he wanted to hear. He leaned in, felt the contours of her body through the vinyl and pressed closer. "Besides, I earned the bragging rights to every one of those hash marks."

She shoved her hand in his face. "Zach, your arrogance is astounding."

"I know," he said with a grin.

Maybe she hadn't meant it as a compliment, but he equated arrogance with self-confidence, and that wasn't exactly a fault in his estimation. "You know you love me." He crowded her by leaning a forearm above his head and against the bulkhead connected to the stall.

She drew the shower curtain tighter, but stood her ground. "Ha!"

"Admit it."

"Not on your life."

He cocked an eyebrow. "What about yours? I'm desperate enough to take a deathbed confession."

She snorted, obviously trying to hold back her laughter. There was nothing delicate about the deep throaty sound.

But he liked it.

"A woman's entitled to her secrets. And I'm definitely taking this one to the grave." Her tone teased him.

Zach relished the torment.

He pressed his advantage while he still had one. "Why not save us both the heartache, sweetheart? Admit it," he murmured, looking deep into her eyes where he could see what she wouldn't confess. She loved him. "We've known each other forever. There are no secrets between us."

Her smile cooled. Her eyes frosted over.

Zach felt a blast of freezer burn.

The Ice Princess was back.

He'd said the wrong thing. Their history went back to the womb. And he had pictures of their pregnant mothers standing side by side to prove it. Their lives were so intertwined he didn't even know where to begin to separate them. Through the years he'd learned to read her like a book. But lately she'd become a mystery, a woman of secrets.

And he'd began to wonder if he really knew her at all.

Lack of persistence was not one of his shortcomings, however. "One of these days you'll realize you can't live without me."

He'd wear her down eventually. Like the minute he popped the question.

He hoped.

"Don't hold your breath."

Why did she have to play so damn hard to get?

Zach leaned in again. "When you figure it out," he whispered close to her ear, "just say where and when and I'll be there with wings on." He backed off, running a hand through his precision military cut and making it stand on end.

All the while her eyes never strayed from his. Their liquid depths held a yearning that equaled his own.

He'd ask. And she'd answer yes.

Feeling reassured, Zach turned to leave, but stopped short with a snap of his fingers. "Almost forgot. We have a preflight briefing in half an hour."

"Why didn't you just say so?"

He made a big show of looking her up and down as if he could see right through the shower curtain. "I had other things on my mind."

It didn't pay a guy to be honest. A bar of soap shot past his ear. It would have hit him square in the jaw if he hadn't ducked when he saw it coming.

With a hearty chuckle, Zach closed the door behind him. He'd have to put in for an increase in hazardous-duty pay once they were married.

And a new assignment.

According to current Navy policy, Michelle couldn't be both his wife and his wingman.

MICHELLE TURNED the cold water all the way up, though it didn't make much difference. There was no such thing as a hot shower with a crew of more than five thousand on board. Still, she wasn't as indifferent to Zach Prince as she pretended. And she needed the cold spray to counter his effect on her libido.

Wouldn't he have been shocked to realize just how much she'd wanted to forget the rules for once? How much she'd wanted to drag him into that tiny shower stall, strip him down to bare rippling muscles, run her hands through jet-black hair and lose herself in sky-blue eyes for two minutes of hot, unbridled sex?

Two minutes, hell. If she had her way, he wouldn't be walking until next Sunday.

She heaved a frustrated sigh. The only reason he professed to want her at all was that he couldn't have her. As soon as the challenge was gone, he would be, too.

He'd done it to others.

And he'd done it to her...

Zach was a dreamer with an innate inability to commit.

Michelle shut off the water with more force than necessary. She'd been waiting forever for him to grow up, mature into the man she wanted him to be—a one-woman man. Not in this lifetime.

At least not during her reproductive years. She felt the familiar stab of regret as she thought wistfully of all she'd given up just to advance this far in her chosen profession.

Reaching for the Navy-issue towel stenciled with her name, Michelle rubbed her skin vigorously. She'd already wasted a dozen or so years thinking herself in love with Zach Prince. It wasn't as if she'd give up flying for him or any man. And then there was the possibility of advancement to lieutenant commander; the shortlist would be out in a few months. With any luck and a lot of hard work her name would be on it.

Love. Who needed it?

Oh, but how easily Zach Prince threw that word around.

I love it when you're riled.

You know you love me. He used that line with every female on board.

Yet he never said those three little words that mattered most.

I love you.

Did he love her? Really?

How could he when he didn't know the true meaning of the word? Tucking the towel in place, she moved to the mirror above the sink. She swiped at the lingering condensation, then confronted her blurred image.

Did she love him?

Even though there wasn't room in her life for anything that wouldn't fit into her already cramped quarters, her heart wanted more. But her head insisted a man wouldn't be worth the complications. So why bother?

Zach, on the other hand, liked the *idea* of being in love. He liked the whirlwind emotions of falling in love. So he fell hard. And often. But he wasn't the kind of guy to be in it for the long haul. He'd get bored and restless...

...and when things got really tough, he wouldn't be there at all.

If she was smart she wouldn't waste another day on him. Or so she kept telling herself over and over. She had her career to think of, a future all carved out that didn't, *couldn't,* include a hotshot pilot like Zach Prince.

Besides...

With her flight physical coming up next month, if she didn't start watching her weight now, she'd be over the maximum for her five-foot-six-inch frame and be given the "NAMI whammy" by the Navel Aerospace and Operational Medical Institute. The slightest imperfections, such as headaches, bad dental work or a few extra pounds, and a pilot would be grounded.

She took great care of her health. She ate right. Exercised. And still carried around an extra ten pounds despite her best efforts. Cover-girl beauty might not be important in the greater scheme of things, but she still realized she didn't have a face that would launch a thousand ships.

Finger-combing her hair, she held it back from her face and gazed at her reflection with a critical eye. "Look at you. Your hair is dirt brown. Your nose is just…there." Not to mention the freckles that made her look about twelve. She attempted a seductive pout, vamping her way out of puberty straight to old maid. "And you look like you've been sucking on a lemon."

Why would Mr. Tall, Dark and Top Gun want you? If she knew the answer to that, maybe she'd believe in his sincerity.

Michelle let go of her hair. It fell past her shoulders to her waist in a cascade of damp waves. Some might think her vain for not cutting it. Short would be so much easier. It would dry faster, too. But short hair required maintenance. And styling products. Not to mention frequent trips to the ship's barber. In the long run, longer hair was the hassle-free choice.

Too much trouble was also the excuse she gave herself for not wearing makeup or perfume, or an assortment of other feminine accoutrements meant to attract men. But then, it wasn't the spotlight she wanted. It was respect.

She wanted the other pilots, especially Zach, to take her seriously. And how was anyone supposed to do that if she spent all her time primping in front of the mirror, instead of poring over flight manuals?

Michelle ran a brush through her wet tangle of hair and secured it in a damp but functional bun, using only a rubber band—stray bobby pins tended to play havoc with a plane's control systems. Now she *felt* more like the pragmatic woman she was.

Moving away from the mirror, she dismissed her image.

Ironic, really, that a woman confident enough to fly multimillion-dollar jets for the military could be so insecure about her appearance.

Of all her unremarkable features, her eyes were probably the only thing she liked about her looks. They were intelligent and hazel-brown. Zach had once remarked they sparkled the exact color of root beer. They'd been kids then and she'd been thirsty for his affection, so she'd foolishly believed him.

Michelle shook her head at the memory, seventeen and wearing her heart on her sleeve. What a mistake.

But she'd learned a lot since that summer.

Such as the only way to keep Zach Prince close was to keep him at arm's length.

THROUGHOUT THE PREFLIGHT briefing in the ready room, Michelle listened intently to Captain Greene, commanding officer of the USS *Enterprise*, as he outlined the upcoming mission for their squadron. She took diligent notes, but occasionally her gaze wandered across the aisle to Zach.

He sat slouched in the comfortable theater-style leather seat, long legs sprawled out in front of him. His slightly lowered eyelids with their thick black lashes gave the impression of boredom. But she knew better. Beneath the facade he remained alert and ready for anything.

As per his usual preflight ritual, he popped a piece of Bazooka in his mouth, the only brand of gum he chewed. Fliers were a superstitious lot and Zach was no exception. He showed the comic strip to his RIO, Ensign Steve Marietta, who went by the call sign Magician. They shared a chuckle. And

Michelle felt a twinge of something in the pit of her stomach.

Jealousy?

She loved to fly with Zach.

They'd been through the academy together. Flight school. Then Fighter Weapons School. And currently assigned to squadron VF-114 out of Miramar, California, as part of the Air Wing assigned to the *Enterprise*.

But her ambition wouldn't allow her to take a back seat to anyone. So it had been a long time since they'd piloted a plane together.

Zach caught her looking at him and winked.

She rolled her eyes with practiced indifference. But the hint of a smile tugged at the corners of her mouth. He took a piece of bubble gum from his upper left pocket and tossed it to her. Disguising the smile, she offered a wry grin in return. He knew she didn't chew the stuff.

She started to stow it in a pocket.

"Open it," he mouthed.

So *that* was it—he wanted her to read the joke. Occasionally he tampered with the cartoons to make them X-rated, although he usually didn't share those with her. Probably because he understood she wouldn't appreciate that brand of humor.

Michelle opened it only to find the cartoon unaltered. Nothing the least bit risqué. She looked at him with a puzzled frown.

His eyebrows drew together as he trained those perfect baby blues on the strip of paper from across the aisle. He turned to Steve and snatched a still-wrapped piece of Bazooka out of the ensign's hand, then tossed the confiscated gum to her.

Michelle raised a questioning eyebrow at his odd behavior.

"Open it," Zach mouthed again.

"Passing notes in class, Prince?" Captain Greene asked.

Heat rushed to Michelle's cheeks. All eyes turned toward her. Skeeter offered a sympathetic smile, but the rest of the room rumbled with male laughter.

She hated the feeling of being under a microscope. As an admiral's daughter she'd lived her whole Navy career that way. As a woman in the macho world of naval aviation she'd had more than her fair share of scrutiny already.

"Perhaps you two would care to share with the rest of us."

"Sure, why not?" Zach offered with his usual nonchalance.

Michelle shook her head at the senior officer's suggestion and tucked the gum into the cargo pocket of her pants leg.

"Good, because this isn't high-school chemistry, and you two aren't teenagers. So keep the raging hormones in check."

As soon as the captain turned his back, Zach tried to get her to go for the gum. She put a hand up to block her peripheral vision and ignored him for the rest of the briefing.

"Any questions?" Captain Greene concluded, clearly anticipating none.

"Yo." Steve raised his hand. "I just thought since we were back in high school..." He got his requisite laugh, then launched into the really stupid stuff everyone expected of him. "I don't think I'm hearing straight. You did say you were giving us two days R&R in Turkey? Would that be a full forty-eight hours, Captain? And where exactly is the nearest strip joint, anyway?"

The room let out a collective groan and bombarded Steve with paper airplanes while the ensign mumbled something about belly dancers and seven veils.

"Magician, you dumbass," Greene admonished. "Figure it out for yourself. If there are no further questions, everyone is dismissed."

"No sweat, Magic Man," Zach said, pushing to his feet. "We'll just fly around until we find one."

They were kidding, of course. At least, she hoped they were. There really was no telling with those two. It irritated her that Zach felt the need to play the dunce when he was probably one of the smartest men she knew. But all too often he hid his intelligence and slid by on his charm. He certainly never had to try as hard as she did.

Flying didn't come easy for her; nothing came easy to a perfectionist. Michelle stood and Zach held up foot traffic to let her and Skeeter pass in front of him.

"I'll spring for the hotel room. First-class all the way," he offered.

"Any other guy would have asked me to dinner first." Michelle tossed the comment over her shoulder as she continued up the aisle.

"But he'd have been thinking about getting you back to his room."

"He's right, you know," Steve piped in. "All I ever think about is getting laid."

Steve grunted and Michelle realized Zach must have given his RIO a well-deserved elbow to the gut. They were boys, both of them, Peter Pans who would never grow up.

And they deserved each other.

What *had* she been thinking? She didn't miss flying with Zach at all.

"If you feel like dinner, we could order up room service," he persisted. "But I was thinking more like breakfast."

"Come on, Skeeter. Let's get out of here," Michelle urged her roommate forward.

"Just do me a favor," Zach whispered. "Read the comic strip—"

"Prince, Dann, a moment of your time." Captain Greene stopped them short.

"Yes, sir." Michelle popped to attention next to Zach while everyone else filed out around them. Within moments there was just the three of them, leaving the ready room unusually quiet.

Normally, pilots were coming and going. Preflight, postflight, the one thing flyboys loved most next to flying was talking about it. It wasn't unusual for them to evaluate each other or own up to mistakes. Especially since a single error could mean the difference between life and death.

She had a niggling suspicion about what was coming.

"At ease," the captain ordered.

Michelle opened her stance, even though she felt far from relaxed. She focused on the captain's bald spot and tried not to think about this little incident getting back to her father. Just like everything else she did.

After the lecture from the captain, she could look forward to one from the admiral.

"Let me start by saying I don't create policy, I just enforce it. I know you kids grew up together and have come through the ranks together, but that doesn't excuse your conduct..."

Michelle could tell by the lack of bluster in Captain Greene's normally booming discourse that he really meant it this time. She found herself tuning out the rest. She knew it by rote. How many times since they were kids had Zach gotten her into trouble by refusing to play by the rules? Even though he somehow always managed to come out smelling like a rose, she took on the distinct odor of Pepe LePew.

She shifted her focus to the "greenie board" over the captain's shoulder. Similar charts hung on the bulkhead of every squadron ready room aboard the ship.

Naval aviation was a competitive field fueled by testosterone. Not only did pilots critique themselves and each other, they were formally graded by a landing signal officer.

Color-coded boxes followed a pilot's last name. Green for an *okay* landing. Yellow, *fair* with some degree of deviation. Red, *no grade* for an ugly approach. Brown, because the pilot had to be waved off due to unsafe conditions. And a blue line meant a "bolter," which was a pilot who'd missed the wires and had to try again.

Not many aviators had the nerves of steel required to touch down on a floating airstrip at full throttle. But if a pilot couldn't land on the deck and not in the drink he was useless to the Navy.

Though LSO scores were subjective, Michelle never lowered herself to lobby for preferential treatment. But one F-14 pilot stood out among the rest.

A line of green followed the name Prince. And it wasn't because he was any better than she at landing the bulky F-14 Tomcats. He was simply a better schmoozer.

Captain Greene droned on. Zach shifted restlessly at her side while Michelle stewed over the yellow block at the end of her green streak.

Fair. She was better than fair.

For that particular landing she'd snagged only the third arresting wire strung across the deck. Sure she'd made a lineup correction at the start of her final pass, settling below the correct approach. But only because the carrier had been late turning into the wind. Flying low as she tried to "chase the lineup" had cost her an okay landing.

Zach never had to settle.

He flew with an instinct she envied. But no one was perfect, especially not Zach Prince.

"This isn't the time or place." Captain Greene's raised voice intruded on her thoughts. "Both of you signed off on that memo I sent around last week, so I'm going to assume you read it. Fraternization among male and female pilots will no longer be tolerated, nor will *any* appearance of impropriety.

"The way I hear it, the two of you make regular treks to each other's quarters. Those visits are to cease and desist at once. Here's how it's going to go down. This time you get off with a warning. Next time it goes in your record. And if it happens a third time—" he paused for effect "—one of you is out of here. Is that understood?"

The two of them?

Once again she'd been lumped together with her rule-breaking running mate. Guilt by association. And she could guess which one of them would be shipping out.

"Aye, aye, sir," they responded in unison.

"You have a job to do. I expect you to do it in a professional manner. That'll be all," he dismissed them. "And Prince," the captain called Zach back. "No more harassing Lieutenant Dann over the airwaves. It doesn't set a good example…"

As the captain continued to rag on Zach, Michelle hurried to the hatch. She'd really had it with Zach this time. Seething with pent-up anger, she didn't trust herself to say two words to the man. And she sure wasn't about to wait around and let him smooth-talk her out of her fit of righteous indignation.

"Michelle!" Zach called from the other end of the narrow passageway, but heavy foot traffic kept him from reaching her.

Ignoring his pleas, she picked up her pace, weaving her way between shipmates.

As she headed toward the ship's elevator, which would take her to the squadron changing room and then up to the flight deck, she cursed herself for being a class-A fool. Captain Greene's warning was a serious one. Fat chance Zach would listen. She'd be better off putting in for a transfer now, before it became compulsory and a smear on her exemplary record.

Damn, Zach.

Why did she always have to be the responsible one?

Michelle pushed the elevator button repeatedly until it finally arrived and passengers emptied out. Then she quickly stepped inside and held down the close-door button.

"Michelle, wait up." Zach reached in and sent the doors sliding in the opposite direction. "Going my way, Lieutenant?" he asked with a sheepish grin as if nothing was wrong.

"Do I have a choice, Lieutenant?" She waited just long enough for the doors to close, shutting off the two of them from curious onlookers. Then she turned and vented her anger by socking him in the arm. "I told you so!"

As the elevator started its ascent, he rubbed his shoulder. With his little-boy charm, he exaggerated the harm she'd inflicted "You don't have to be so smug about it."

"Smug? Because you'll receive a slap on the wrist while I'll get booted out of the Navy? If you won't think about your career, at least think about mine. Do you have any idea how serious this is? We were lucky to get off with just a warning." She faced forward and folded her arms.

"I know how serious I am about us..." The doors started to part. He moved to the control panel and held down the close-door button despite the rumble of protest from those waiting outside the elevator.

Because he stood directly in her line of vision she had no choice but to look at him. He stared at her with such burning intensity it would have been hard for her to ignore him, but whatever the promise in his eyes, she didn't want to see it.

"There is no 'us,' Zach."

"There's always been an 'us,' Michelle."

She could almost hear the sincerity in the deep baritone of his voice. But it only made her want to lash out, inflict more pain until he was feeling as conflicted as she felt every time she looked at him, every time she got behind the controls of her Tomcat. There was no room in her life for the two things she wanted most.

In the end she could only have one.

She knew what to expect from a machine. Her expectations for this particular man could only lead to heartbreak. The ability to compartmentalize one's mind was a critical skill for a pilot. Zach didn't fit neatly into any aspect of her life. Friend, boyfriend? Lover, squad leader?

Competition.

She had no option left but to cut him out completely.

"Get it into that thick skull of yours, Prince. *I don't love you!* I've never loved you. Why can't you just leave me alone?" She batted his hand away from the hold button and fled as the doors slid open. She didn't wait to hear if maybe, just maybe, his answer would give her the one thing she didn't need right now.

Hope.

CHAPTER TWO

LEAVE HER ALONE? Zach stood in the wake of Michelle's words and his own total disbelief. Like hell he would!

He was just about to start after her when the elevator began to fill up around him, bringing him back to his senses. She needed space. And he needed...damn, he couldn't think of anything he needed except her.

He changed direction midstep. Jostling a senior officer on the way out, Zach mumbled a hasty apology. The commander growled something in return. Great, that probably cost him a grade on his next landing. The guy had a reputation for being a hard-ass LSO. But Zach didn't feel like sucking up today.

He turned aft down the amidships passageway toward the nearest officers' mess. He'd long since chewed the sugar out of his gum, but he punctuated his thoughts by snapping bubbles in rapid-fire succession.

Michelle had brought him as close as he'd ever

come to losing his cool. As a rule, he had the easygoing nature of a middle child. With an overachiever for an older sister, he'd naturally learned to keep up or get left behind. And because his kid brother worshiped the ground he walked on, he'd made sure the squirt came along for the ride. They were a competitive family.

But with Michelle, it was just that much easier to let her be the boss. He didn't mind taking the back seat in their as-yet-undefined relationship. What he did mind was being dumped out on the highway at ninety miles an hour, mowed down and left as roadkill.

I don't love you! I've never loved you. Why can't you just leave me alone?

He didn't believe her, but something was definitely wrong. She'd grown distant these past few months. He could feel her slipping away with each passing day. And he didn't know how to hold on. So he'd taken the action of a man desperate and damned.

He'd bought an engagement ring.

Duty free. Right out of the *Navy Exchange Catalog*. Zach almost groaned out loud thinking about his lack of sensibility. He considered himself a pretty smart guy. He knew better than to purchase a diamond sight unseen.

For one thing it didn't have any romantic appeal. The parcel had arrived yesterday at mail call—

dripping wet after the helicopter had dropped a couple of mailbags into the ocean during transfer. The bundles had been retrieved by divers. Postal clerks had somehow managed to sort through illegible ink smears and soaked care packages to find their disgruntled recipients.

When he'd taken the ring from the soggy box, the plain gold band with its substandard crystallized carbon looked just about perfect nestled in the palm of his hand. From that moment on he couldn't wait to slip the logical, if somewhat flawed, token of his esteem onto Michelle's finger.

Hell, he could always buy her a bigger rock. And he'd have a lifetime to get used to the idea of being married.

Marriage. A big step. Maybe the biggest he'd take in his lifetime. Making the decision to leap felt kind of like an emergency ejection during an aborted takeoff. Damned if you did, and damned if you didn't. Odds were you'd survive a crash in front of the ship only to be dragged under and drowned.

And that was what he felt like right now. A drowning man. But Michelle was his life preserver.

As he neared the mess, the deceptive smells of sizzling bacon and frying eggs—any-way-you-like-'em as long as you liked them runny and scrambled—ambushed his senses. There hadn't been eggs on board since the last port of call.

Above the cacophony of sounds from the busy kitchen and several simultaneous conversations from the dining area, he zeroed in on his RIO's street-smart, New York accent.

"Yo, Zach! Over here." Steve waved from a corner cloth-covered table where he sat eating breakfast with Skeeter. The white linen was supposed to remind them they were officers. And somehow make them forget they were eating the same chow as the enlisted personnel.

Zach nodded as he entered and picked up a tray. Moving quickly through the breakfast buffet line, he chose his favorite preflight carbo load—a short stack of pancakes drowned in imitation maple syrup with a tall glass of powdered milk on the side.

God, he missed whole milk, fresh eggs and a long grocery list of other favorite foods. But this far into deployment just about everything came reconstituted.

Welcome to shipboard life, *haze gray and under way.*

Plastering a smile on his face, Zach pulled out a chair next to Skeeter and sat down.

"The old man rip you a new one?" Steve asked.

"You could say that," Zach admitted "Where's Michelle?"

"I've already had this conversation once today and it's not even 0600. He's all yours, Marietta."

Skeeter got up, leaving the rest of her breakfast untouched.

Plucking the dusty plastic rose from the bud vase, Zach held it out to her. "Are you sure you have to go?"

Skeeter rejected the faux flower and his insincerity by turning away.

"I don't think she likes me," Zach confided in his RIO once the other navigator was out of earshot. Not that he cared. Sticking his gum on the side of his plate, he picked up his glass.

"Aren't you barking up the wrong skirt?"

Zach almost choked on a swallow of chalky milk headed down his windpipe. He coughed to clear his throat.

Steve offered a sheepish grin. "So Skeeter doesn't like you and Michelle is pissed at you—what else is new?" Steve sopped up the gravy on his plate with his last bite of biscuit, a Navy specialty called SOS.

"'Pissed' is an understatement." Zach dug into his pancakes. "Michelle acts as if I'm out to destroy her career," he managed to say between bites.

"And you probably will. Admit it, Prince, you're a nonconformist. You don't give a damn about your career. But you're a helluva F-14 pilot, which is why the Navy puts up with you. Your call sign isn't Renegade for nothing, you know."

"Yeah, I know." Even before this latest ass-chewing, he'd been thinking about what he had to offer the Navy and what he wanted in return. But despite what anyone thought, it bothered him that Michelle thought he was out to destroy her life when all he wanted to do was be a part of it. Maybe he'd have been better off following in his father's footsteps to the SEAL teams, instead of pursuing Michelle into aviation.

He loved to fly, but his laid-back approach in a world that moved at Mach II sometimes made him look indolent. Maybe he'd be better off out of the service altogether. "If I start submitting my résumé now—"

"Whoa. Back up." Steve pushed aside his plate. "You want to fly for a commercial airline?"

"Why not? I'm at the end of my obligated service. I could have a civilian job by the end of the cruise."

It was no secret the airlines recruited military pilots right out of flight school. He and Michelle could both easily get *real* jobs. Was that what he wanted to do with the rest of his life? A commuter run between Sioux Falls and Cedar Rapids? Two point five kids? A white picket fence?

He wasn't sure.

But sometime during the past four months the idea had taken hold and wouldn't let go. Now all he had to do was convince Michelle.

"Wipe those thoughts right out of your head. Talk about conforming—" Steve reached for Skeeter's bowl of unfinished cereal and started shoveling soggy shredded wheat into his mouth "—that is not what's going to make you happy, my friend." Steve let his less-than-objective opinion be known between swallows of slop. Zach was used to his friend's garbage gut and his convictions.

Steve's eyesight had kept him from becoming a pilot and fulfilling his own dream of becoming a Blue Angel, the Navy's elite exhibition fliers. Even after laser surgery corrected his vision, the Navy rejected his request to retrain from a designated NFO—naval flight officer—to a pilot. Retreads, as the Navy liked to call them, had a higher percentage of crashes. But that didn't stop Steve from trying to cut through the red tape, however.

"Don't take it personally, Magic Man. You're the best radar I've ever had in my back seat. And you'd make one helluva pilot. Even Greene is pulling for you on this one."

Beyond that, Zach didn't offer any encouragement. Whether or not Steve would ever find himself behind the controls of a jet all depended on the needs of the Navy.

"You can't be serious about giving up jets, Prince."

Do you have any idea how serious this is? We were lucky to get off with just a warning.

"I've never been more serious about anything in my life." *Or anyone.* His deepest personal thought caught the tail end of his sentence and went along for the ride.

It didn't matter what he did as long as they were together.

If he and Michelle married while in the service, they'd see less of each other than they did now. There'd be long separations. Restrictions when they were together. And he didn't have a clue how they'd ever manage a family. But if he could convince her they had other options...

The ensign leaned forward in his seat. "Take my advice, Prince. Forget about it. You're a naval aviator, there's JP-5 running through your veins. If the Navy wanted guys like us to have families, they'd have issued a wife and kids along with the seabag."

Steve spoke the truth. Not too very long ago the Navy hadn't even allowed married men to train as pilots. Single guys were discouraged from tying the knot. Firstborn sons from two-parent families with stay-at-home mothers and domineering fathers were considered ideal candidates, according to one Navy study, because of their natural arrogance.

Opportunities for women, once nonexistent,

were just now opening up. Michelle's pride was all wrapped up in being among the first female fighters. And he was going to ask her to give that up?

She'd never go for it. Even he had to admit how much she loved flying.

What had he done?

"I appreciate the warning, Magic Man. But it's too late." He'd already popped the question, so to speak. But he was no longer sure about her answer.

A CORNER OF the squadron changing room was sectioned off by a hanging bedsheet. The easy locker-room banter subsided as Michelle entered, then picked up again as she crossed to the other side of the jerry-rigged drape.

Since her introduction to the Fighting Aardvarks of VF-114, she'd seen as much of these men as their wives and proctologists. Yet the barriers remained.

The partition only served as a reminder.

It certainly wasn't there to protect her already compromised modesty.

Michelle grabbed her G suit from its hook and put it on over her flight suit. In the post-Tailhook era male fliers acted with caution around their female counterparts. When asked, they dutifully acknowledged women as their equals, but resentment brewed beneath the surface.

Michelle shut out thoughts of equality as she

shrugged into her survival vest. She had a job to do. The same as the men. For better or worse, for now at least, she was a Vark.

Hearing Zach's familiar voice from the other side of the curtain, she realized he'd come into the room and wasn't attempting to sweet-talk her out of her bad mood. In fact, he ignored her altogether as he carried on a conversation about weather conditions with the rest of the guys.

Michelle paused in putting on her gear.

What did she expect? She'd made it clear she wanted him to leave her alone. Even if deep down that wasn't what she wanted at all. She'd made her choice, the right choice, and now she had to live with it. Still, it would be tough going on without him. He'd always been a part of her world.

He'd smoothed over the rough waters of squadron life. And she credited him with the fact that the men even tolerated her at all. His easy acceptance of her as his wingman made them all more comfortable.

It was her job to ride his wing. Follow his orders. But she'd always felt as if he didn't mind being the one watching out for her, something she didn't always appreciate, but remained grateful for nonetheless.

There were pilots who considered it bad luck to have a woman walk the wings of their parked planes, let alone ride in them.

Michelle's gaze involuntarily darted to an eye-level rip in the sheet, searching for Zach on the other side. Some smart-ass had printed the words *peep show* in Magic Marker on the guy side. Skeeter had retaliated by drawing the male symbol around the hole, the arrow pointing to the words *no show* on the gal side.

Even though Skeeter was only on her first carrier cruise, she could hold her own with this bunch of bandits.

When she realized what she was doing, Michelle forced herself to look away. If they caught her peeking, she'd never hear the end of it.

Well, that would be one way to lose her icy reputation. Though she'd hate to think of what they'd call her then. Behind her back the Varks referred to her as the Ice Princess. Which was fine. Because the one thing they'd never call her was Quota Queen.

She'd earned her gold wings. And the price she'd paid may very well have been her only chance at happiness. Certainly it was higher than the price paid by a man.

Bending over in an exaggerated bow, she cinched her parachute harness tight, reminding herself of at least one advantage to being a woman. She didn't have to worry about crushing her balls during an emergency ejection.

Sweeping aside the curtain, she strode past the

men with all the regal bearing of a condemned royal, pausing only long enough to pick up her oxygen mask and helmet with the call sign Rapunzel emblazoned across the front.

A flight instructor had given her the tag after her first solo. In the aftermath of excitement, she'd taken off her helmet and let down her hair.

A mistake she'd never make again.

ON THE FLIGHT DECK, winds buffeted Michelle's face. Jet engines roared in her ears and rattled her teeth, while the familiar heady scent of jet fumes filled her nostrils.

The sun put in its first appearance of the day, highlighting the light cloud cover with streaks of bright orange and pink.

A fine Navy day, as her father would say.

God, she loved this life. Nothing compared with a dawn launch off an aircraft carrier. She'd take that adrenaline rush over a man any day.

Pausing to check the safety of her 9-mm pistol, she placed the gun back in the holster pocket of her survival vest. Then ran a confident hand across the sleek underbelly of her assigned F-14 Tomcat. This was the point when she pushed aside all self-doubt and donned the persona of Xena Warrior Princess.

"I read the maintenance log," Skeeter shouted above the din as she joined in the preflight walk-through. "The last pilot reported a problem with the left rudder, but the ground crew didn't find anything."

"Thanks, I'll check it out." Even though she trusted the "Vark fixers," Michelle didn't believe in leaving anything to chance. As a Navy pilot, she knew her plane inside and out.

Circling the aircraft, Michelle scanned the overall structural integrity of the jet. After she inspected the hydraulic gauges, she moved on to check the tires. And more importantly, she made sure the tailhook was pointed down. If the hook couldn't catch the arresting wire and the jet couldn't be diverted to a land base, the pilot had to fly into a steel-mesh-and-canvas-net barricade strung across the deck. A terrifying experience she could do without.

"You okay? You seem distracted," Skeeter observed.

"Well, you know Captain Greene."

"That bad, huh?"

"Worse."

"I thought maybe you and Zach had a fight."

Michelle didn't respond at first, needing the few moments it took to round the plane and come up on the nose again. But finally she had to satisfy her curiosity. "What makes you think Zach and I are fighting?"

"For one thing," Skeeter answered, "he keeps

looking over here with those soulful blue eyes of his.''

Michelle feigned indifference, but from the look on her RIO's face, Skeeter wasn't buying it. She pushed on the nose of the Tomcat to make sure the cone wouldn't flip up during the catapult launch and crack the windshield.

Her gaze darted toward Zach's plane a few feet away. They made eye contact from where he crouched on the wing checking an access panel. But he didn't offer a jaunty salute or wave as he normally would have.

The corner of her mouth turned up in a sad smile. "He always looks like that."

"Maybe when he looks at you. Personally, I don't know what you see in him," Skeeter said.

"Nothing," Michelle denied automatically. Skeeter was probably the only person she knew who wasn't taken in by Zach's charisma. "In fact, I'm putting in for a transfer when we get to Turkey. I'm thinking about joining the Nintendo generation and retraining to fly the F/A-18 Hornet," Michelle confided. The thought hadn't even occurred to her until she shaded her eyes to watch as one of the newer, more maneuverable jets landed on deck.

The pilots were younger, from a generation where working mothers were the norm, and less likely to see a female flier as a threat. Hell, as sobering as the thought was, they'd probably think of her as mom.

Motherhood. With thirty approaching at Mach speed, she couldn't deny thinking about it a time or two lately. Mostly with regret for what would never be.

A son with dark hair and blue eyes, toddling after his daddy...or a daughter, slipping her tiny hand into a much larger one...

"What about an F-14 squadron on the East Coast?" Skeeter asked.

A tidal wave of homesickness washed over Michelle for her home state of Virginia. For her mom and dad.

For forfeit fantasies.

"You don't really want to fly with Bitchin' Betty, instead of me, do you?" Skeeter persisted.

Michelle forced her attention back to her RIO, who was referring to the soft feminine voice of the computer system in the newer aircraft. The Hornet and the Super Hornet didn't need a navigator. The pilot viewed operating systems from a four-inch screen with a touch pad, instead of having to scan countless dials and gauges.

The jet was equipped to do the job of two planes—the fighter and the attack bomber—while utilizing only one-quarter of the personnel. In a few short years fighters like the F-14 Tomcat would be as obsolete as bombers like the A-6 Intruder. And so would she. Why hadn't she seen the writing on the wall sooner?

"If you stayed with the F-14, I could ship out with you." Skeeter sounded a little desperate. And no wonder. As a pilot, Michelle had more options than her flight officer did. An NFO qualified to ride in, but not drive, a plane.

In Skeeter's case, she was too short. Skeeter had received a waiver for the back seat only after proving she could reach the farthest control, the handle that jettisoned the canopy during an emergency ejection.

The Navy had built its planes decades earlier to accommodate males from five-six to six-three. Michelle's height and build worked in her favor. "You'd want to do that?" she asked, weighing Skeeter's feelings against her own motives. She didn't want to hurt her dear friend with careless words or deeds. It wasn't necessary to make up her mind right now.

"We're a team, right?"

"Teammates," Michelle agreed, but wondered in the end if she wouldn't be moving on. She stole another glance at Zach, gabbing with a grape, a person wearing the purple vest of aviation fuels. The young enlisted woman appeared to hang on his every word. The knot in Michelle's stomach tightened.

She knew what that girl and others saw when

they looked at Zach, his movie-star looks for one thing. The charm that radiated from every pore for another.

But what did *she* see in him? Nothing…

Except that he was everything she wasn't. A better pilot. A better person. And she resented him for it. And some resentments took a lifetime to overcome.

Michelle climbed onto the left wing to check the rudder. Was it possible to be jealous of *and* in love with your best friend?

WITH ONE LAST LOOK in Michelle's direction, Zach put on his helmet and pulled down the visor, then climbed into the cockpit of his Tomcat.

It was already too late for his heart. And as soon as she got around to that piece of bubble gum in her pocket, it'd be too late for his pride.

He had nothing left to lose. Except her friendship.

Why hadn't he left well enough alone?

Why did this restlessness he felt have him acting on impulse? He should have waited. Until her birthday, at least. By then maybe he'd have come to his senses. He'd waited four months already, since the ship left port, and that wasn't exactly impulsive. Hell, who was he kidding? He'd had this particular itch for more than twelve years. He'd just been too spineless to scratch it before now. So why then, when he'd finally worked up the courage, was he breaking out in hives?

Steve climbed into the back seat and closed them off inside the Plexiglas canopy. Zach hooked up his G suit, oxygen mask and fastened the torso harness of his ejection seat. With a map strapped to the top of one knee and a scratch pad with notes secured to the other, he cinched the straps that held his legs in position. Flailing appendages could get chopped off in an emergency ejection.

Some pilots liked the snug feeling, but it made him feel claustrophobic, at least until he was airborne and could forget about the harness altogether.

He fired up the jet engines.

"You sure you want to give all this up?" Steve asked from behind him as they slowly taxied to the launch, following the taxi director's signal. Hands above the waist were for the pilot, below were for the ground crew.

Zach smiled to himself. "I'm sure." It wouldn't be easy. But either way his life would never be the same.

That was why he'd stopped by Greene's office and submitted a request for SEAL training. If Michelle didn't want to marry him, there'd be no use hanging around the Air Wing.

They were launching from one of two forward positions today. Rapunzel and Skeeter from the other. The trip to Turkey wasn't all fun and games. They'd meet up with allied forces for a week of training exercises before earning their forty-eight hours of liberty.

That gave him between takeoff and landing to convince Michelle to come along for the ride of her life. He pulled his lucky charm from his pocket, a photo of them together at Top Gun graduation. Removing the wad of gum from his mouth, he stuck it to the back of the picture and fixed it to the dashboard.

As he taxied into the catapult position, a square of deck angled up to deflect exhaust. A yellow vest—a catapult launch officer with Mickey Mouse ears to protect his hearing—signaled for him to extend the launch bar. Zach obliged and crewmen scurried underneath to hook the bar to the track. Zach pushed the throttle forward to full power.

The jet shuddered as the engines roared.

He ran an automatic check of his control stick and rudder pedals as he eyeballed the panels and gauges.

So far, so good.

Zach switched the launch bar to the retract setting, then grabbed the catapult hand grip in his left hand and locked his elbow. Releasing the wheel brakes, he braced his heels against the floor so he wouldn't accidentally tap a rudder pedal.

The launch bar tightened. The nose dipped. And the launch officer took over.

Zach's blood pumped with anticipation. He gripped the joystick with his right hand, but wouldn't have control of the Tomcat until they were clear of the bow.

"Ready to rock and roll." Zach gave the launch officer a sharp salute.

Like a projectile propelled from a slingshot, the Tomcat took to the horizon. Zach's eyes remained glued to the gauges, when they weren't rolling back into his head. His helmet stayed pinned to the headrest and his stomach was up somewhere near his throat. But his adrenaline hummed, then sang as the F-14 shot from the boat.

He had exactly two seconds for the jet to reach 120 knots; if it didn't, he'd pull the yellow cord between his legs. Ejecting in front of the ship could be as dangerous as failing to eject. Being keel-hauled, dragged under a 130-foot-long beam held little appeal. And little chance for survival.

God, he was going to miss this.

"We're clear!" Steve whooped from the back seat, knowing the microphones to the tower weren't keyed up yet.

As Zach took control of the stick, the dawn promised a clear azure sky and miles of visibility. Pink cotton-candy clouds overhead and bottomless blue ocean below gave him a sense of freedom that was hard to define. Since that very first day he'd taken to the sky, he knew it was where he belonged. Just as he knew he and Michelle belonged together.

As a fighter pilot he had to possess the right combination of nerves and daring to take off and land a thirty-eight-million-dollar jet on a moving airstrip about the size of a football field.

Not to mention a little bit of attitude.

Zach had all three in abundance.

The one thing he didn't have was the girl. And he intended to rectify that very soon.

"Tomcat Leader, this is Two. I've got your 'six' covered,'' Michelle reported in on the tower frequency, having launched right behind him.

" 'Anytime, baby,' '' Zach quoted the Tomcat motto. "Angels nineteen, recommend two-twenty,'' he called back.

"Copy, Tomcat Leader. Cruising altitude nineteen thousand feet. Airspeed 220 knots,'' she rattled off the nautical miles in her soft alto static. "Two, on the way to heaven.''

"Roger, Two, I'll meet you there.''

Zach eased back on the stick, taking the Tomcat up to their designated rendezvous as he wondered what the view was like from a jumbo jet. "This is your captain speaking,'' he said into his mouthpiece. "The temperature in Istanbul is a balmy seventy-two degrees.... In a few minutes you'll see

Saudi Arabia coming up on your left, and to the right, Iraq.

"Your stewardess, Steve, will be around with peanuts and all the booze your kidneys can hold. Thank you for flying Renegade Air."

"Practicing?" Steve asked.

"Thought it might be a good idea." Maybe he'd be able to convince Michelle there were friendlier skies where they *could* be together.

"There's something I gotta ask you, Rapunzel."

"Not today, Renegade. I'm not in the mood."

"PMS with wings," Steve shared on the back mike.

"I was just wondering how you felt about United."

"United? The airline?" Michelle asked.

"Renegade!" Captain Greene's bellow vibrated through his helmet. "I'll bust your butt all the way down to seaman recruit if you keep talking like that."

"Aye, aye, sir."

"Smart-ass," Greene shot back.

"That's an affirmative, Captain." Zach chuckled. The captain liked a good verbal spar as much as he did—only, the senior officer had the rank to back up his bluster.

"Right now I've got a bigger problem than your mouth, hotshot. I've got a broken catapult and a plane in the drink. Next launch in ten..." The captain paused to listen for the report, then let out a string of expletives. "Make that twenty."

"Roger, twenty. One and Two going on alone." Zach hoped the poor bastards whose jet had taken a nosedive into the water lived to tell about it.

Their flight path would take them over the Persian Gulf into the coalition-enforced no-fly zone over southern Iraq, where they'd do a little policing for Kuwait. Then over Saudi Arabia, Jordan and Syria until they reached their destination, Turkey.

"Copy." Michelle acknowledged the message.

Zach switched to the prearranged frequency that would keep their cockpit conversations private just in time to hear Michelle chewing him out.

"Must you provoke him like that?" she demanded.

Michelle took Captain Greene a lot more seriously than he did. She took *life* a lot more seriously. So how did he prove he was serious enough about her to take on more responsibility? She'd be good for him. And he'd be good for her. Why couldn't she see that?

"Rapunzel, Rapunzel, let down your hair."

"Are you calling me uptight?"

"If the shoe fits."

"Now you're mixing up your fairy tales. That's 'Cinderella.'"

Zach chuckled. "United. Think about it. Lead's breaking for a G warm-up." He banked the jet right ninety degrees, diving one thousand feet in a 4G maneuver to test his reaction times.

Four times the force of gravity meant he now weighed eight hundred pounds and his movements were harder to control. When the aircraft's weight sensor detected the increase, air from the engine rushed in, inflating his anti-G suit and squeezing the lower half of his body to keep blood pumping to his brain and to keep him from passing out. No one could ever accuse a jet pilot of thinking with his lower extremities.

At least not while flying.

"Renegade, checks out okay," Zach reported.

"Magician, okay."

"Two breaking." Michelle followed his lead.

Zach gave her enough time to pull off the stunt, but she didn't report back right away. "Two?"

"Roger. Skeeter, okay."

"Rapunzel, okay."

She'd hesitated a moment too long. "Two?" he asked again.

"Let's put the pedal to the metal," she responded.

"Negative, Two." A body reacted differently to the G force from one day to the next. And as far as he knew, she'd skipped breakfast. As squad leader, if he suspected a serious physical impairment to her flying, he could order her back to the carrier. She wouldn't like it. But he'd do it. "Run through that G warm-up again."

"What—"

"Humor me. That's an order, Two."

"Two breaking for *another* G warm-up," she answered back with a little too much sass.

Just the way he liked it.

Zach craned his neck to watch her jet bank, then dive against the backdrop of blue sky.

"Rapunzel, checks out okay," she reported back, right away this time.

"Skeeter, okay."

"Copy, Two. Recommend Mach I." The speed of sound.

"Roger, Tomcat leader. I concur."

Zach maintained a somber mood for the rest of the flight. It went against his nature, but playtime was over. They were without backup. And it wasn't that long ago he'd been a raw ensign flying sorties over Iraq. That thought was enough to sober him up fast.

F-14 Tomcats were fighters. So he hadn't participated in bombing runs. Though he'd thrilled to the experience of hair-raising dives and recoveries in trainers, he wouldn't trade his fighter for a bomber or the new fighter/attack bomber like the F/A-18 Hornet for the world.

It would be even worse than a jumbo jet.

Give him a good dogfight any day, the last arena

of gentleman warfare. There were rules of engagement, and both pilots had chosen to be there.

"Tomcat Leader, this is Tower. We have a bogey 800 knots and closing."

"Single?" Zach queried the tower and his RIO at the same time. "Magic Man?"

"Got him on the screen," Steve answered first. "Looks like a single."

"I see him, too," Skeeter reported.

"Eyes open," Zach ordered.

"One o'clock, MiG-28. Headed straight for us," Steve supplied as the more maneuverable Russian-made aircraft bearing the red, white and black colors of Iraq broke through the clouds and into their line of vision.

Nothing to lose his breakfast over, Zach surmised. Since the Gulf War, Iraqi and American fighters did everything they could to avoid confrontation with one another. Zach didn't expect today to be any different.

"He's not supposed to be in the no-fly zone. Let's chase him home," he ordered, maneuvering his jet into a split S, a quick U-turn that would bring him in low on the bogey. He craned his head to the left as he turned right.

"Copy. Got you covered, Tomcat Leader." Michelle followed his lead.

Dogfighting had changed little since WWI, but it wasn't as easy as it looked on the big screen.

First you had to get in the control zone, the cone behind the other jet. And you could only attack from the same angle of plane. A dogfight lasted all of sixty seconds or less. After that first minute survival rates dropped dramatically.

At any given moment a pilot handled a dozen or more calculations in his head. In training they practiced juggling tennis balls and solving mathematical equations at the same time. A well-trained fighter pilot's instincts were so honed he could fly without thinking and concentrate on making split-second decisions.

The MiG pilot had enough maneuvers to keep them on the edge of their seats as they raced through the skies at speeds that exceeded the sound barrier.

"This guy's pissin' me off. Why isn't he leaving the zone?" Zach questioned the Iraqi pilot's motives. "Let's see if we can get him to panic and run." He zeroed in on the target. "I've got a lock!" The beep of the HUD—heads-up display— confirmed it. "He's bugging out." The MiG sped ahead just as alarms blared in the cockpit. "Shit! Surface-to-air missiles." They were about to cross over into Iraqi airspace.

"Radar's trying to get a lock," Steve confirmed.

"We've got bells going off here," Michelle warned.

"Bug out!" Zach ordered as he switched to evasive tactics.

"Affirmative." Michelle took the lead in the turn.

"Renegade, MiG's in pursuit," Steve informed him.

"What does this guy think he's doing?" They were back in the coalition controlled airspace, the no-fly zone over southern Iraq and Kuwait.

Something wasn't right. Zach felt it in his gut.

If this was all for shits and giggles, the MiG pilot would have bugged out by now. This guy was playing cat-and-mouse as if he wanted to get caught. Which could mean only one thing—this MiG was the cheese. So they'd better keep their eyes open for more enemy fighters.

"Tower, this is Tomcat Leader—"

"Keep your cool, hotshot," Captain Greene broke in with instructions. "See if you can lead him out over the gulf."

"How much fuel do we have, Magic Man?"

"Not enough for this shit," Steve answered even before calculating the amount of fuel in exact pounds. Dogfighting was the difference between a Sunday drive and drag racing when it came to fuel consumption.

"Keep an eye on it for me. Copy, Tower. Two, whaddya say we make a MiG sandwich. Can you get behind this guy?"

"Affirmative. I'm pulling around behind."

"Renegade, two more bogeys closing in," Steve warned.

"Copy. What'd Iraq do—send up their whole damn air farce today?" The Iraqi fighters wouldn't be led out to sea, and keeping the three jets out of southern Iraq and away from Kuwait forced them all deeper into the Republic of Iraq. But every time the Tomcats gave up chase the Iraqi fighters came back around. "Tower, recommend radio Saudi for some backup from the Air Force."

"Negative. We've launched four of our own. ETA, ten minutes. By the time the Air Force gets off the ground, we'd already be there."

"We've got two bogeys on our tail," Skeeter reported.

"Gotcha covered." Zach slammed on the air brakes. Pulling back hard on the stick, he maneuvered the jet in an over-the-top back flip known as an Immelmann—named after the WWI German flying ace who'd invented it.

Then he rolled in behind the lag MiG.

Lag pursuit required a patience Zach didn't possess right now. He opted for lead pursuit. Taking a high yo-yo shortcut through the other pilot's circle, he cut off bogey number three from Michelle.

Meanwhile, she lured the MiG directly behind her into a rolling scissors, a dizzying Ferris-wheel form of pure pursuit that pulled as much as eight

G's. But with a little luck and a lot of skill she would eventually put her Tomcat behind the MiG.

That took care of bogey number two.

And left number one, the lead MiG open to come in behind either him or Michelle. Zach was the easier target. He made sure he kept it that way.

Everything happened fast and furious with three MiGs and two Tomcats vying to lock on to enemy craft. Zach's head moved on a swivel, trying to keep up with his jet. Steve rattled in his ears, tracking both friend and foe.

Michelle dropped below two thousand feet before she managed to get into the cone zone of MiG Two. As soon as she did, MiG One lined up behind her.

"He's trying to get a lock." She sounded composed and in control, pulling from her bag of tricks a countermaneuver for every maneuver the MiG tried.

God, she was good.

The way she kept her cool made him hot all over. "Shake your tail feathers, baby," Zach ordered. He wanted her safe. And he wasn't about to play games with her life. "Tower, where's that backup?"

"ETA, eight minutes."

"We're over Iraqi-controlled airspace," Steve warned.

G's slammed Zach's body. Winds buffeted the

plane. Alarms rang in the cockpit and throughout his head.

"He's got a lock." Michelle put her Tomcat into a barrel roll, launching chaff and flares to confuse any heat-seeking missiles. "I can't shake him."

"I'm lining up right behind him." Zach had two MiGs on his tail now. The one directly behind him locked on. He launched a confusing barrage of chaff and stuck like glue to the MiG riding Rapunzel's six.

The bogey kept on her.

Sweat gushed from every pore of his body, soaking through his flight suit as he sucked down oxygen from his face mask.

Hold him off, sweetheart.

Lock on, lock on, he demanded of himself.

The HUD showed the bogey in the "pickle" and beeped. "Yes! Enough of this shit. Tower, I've got a lock." Zach's thumb hovered over the trigger of the Sidewinder, a close-range air-to-air combat missile. "Permission to fire."

"Do not engage," Captain Greene spouted policy. They were not to fire unless fired upon.

"He's all over Rapunzel's ass!"

Then it happened. His worst nightmare.

The MiG fired, scoring a direct hit.

The tail of Michelle's Tomcat burst into flames. Her plane spiraled toward the ground.

"Eject! Eject, dammit!" Zach shouted.

CHAPTER THREE

One month later
LIEUTENANT PRINCE'S OFF-BASE RESIDENCE,
Miramar, CA

"EJECT, eject, dammit!" Zach awoke with a start. Heart thumping, sweat beading his forehead, he kicked free of the tangled sheets to sit on the edge of the mattress.

The glaring red numbers of the electric alarm clock on the nightstand flashed twelve noon.

He didn't give a rat's ass what time it was, or what day, for that matter. If it wasn't for the nightmares, he'd just as soon stay in bed. With a shaking hand, he reached for the half-empty bottle of bourbon, poured two fingers into a dirty glass and slammed it down in one swallow.

Resting his head in his palms, he tried to keep the forming headache at bay while the liquor burned a hole straight through his gut.

The pounding in his head became insistent before he realized someone was knocking at the door.

"Go away!" he shouted. He realized his mistake when the echo of his words reverberated throughout his aching head.

The pounding persisted. He could hear doors opening and closing up and down the breezeway as neighbors added their complaints. Great. Just great.

"Keep your socks on," he grumbled, searching for something to cover his bare butt. "I'm coming!"

Zach found a pair of boxer briefs, discarded near the foot of the bed and stepped into them. He needed a shave. He needed a shower. And he had no idea where the rest of his clothes were until he tripped over them on the way to answer the door.

Wanting to connect his fist with whomever waited on the other side, Zach flung open the door. A naval officer stood on the stoop.

"Shit!" Zach eyeballed his brother-in-law, Marc Miller, with the shiny new rank of captain pinned to the collar points of his khaki uniform. "What do you want?"

Zach turned his back on the other man and headed straight for the waiting bottle. He'd managed to avoid his family for the better part of the past month. He'd even unplugged his phone.

But they must have decided to send in reinforcements. The last thing he wanted or needed right now was his family descending on him. When Miller didn't speak, Zach was forced to turn around and look at him.

"You didn't show up for rehab," Miller said at last, closing the door behind him.

Zach tipped the bottle to the glass. "So I'm a couple hours late. Can you blame a guy for one last binge?"

"Must have been one hell of a party." Miller scowled at the pizza boxes and other remnants of fast-food trash scattered around the place. "You're two days late. You were supposed to report to the naval hospital in San Diego on Wednesday. It's Friday."

"Hours, days. So I'm late. Is that what you came to tell me? Message delivered." Zach offered a mock salute with the bottle.

Miller didn't look the least bit amused. "The thing is…you're all out of chances, Prince. Those billets in rehab are reserved for personnel who really want them."

"What the hell. It doesn't matter." He set the bottle aside and clung to the glass.

"Probably not," Miller agreed. "But by not showing up you're UA—unauthorized absence, in case you forgot. Good thing for you you've got friends in high places. If it was up to me, I'd leave you to wallow in your self-pity. But you're right,

I'm just the messenger. So here it is.'' Miller handed him a folded piece of paper. "Orders to SEAL training starting Monday, 0700.''

Zach took the orders, but didn't bother to read them. He'd forgotten about submitting the request. It didn't matter now, anyway. He had no intention of falling back on the family tradition of becoming a Navy SEAL, commando of sea, air and land. His father had been a notorious Navy SEAL frogman before his retirement. His sister, Tabby, had become the very first female SEAL. And his brother-in-law was the commanding officer in charge of SEAL training.

No way in hell would he subject himself to that.

He was already in hell. And like Miller said, he was out of options. He'd sabotaged rehab because he couldn't stand the thought of opening a vein and bleeding his emotions in front of fellow substance abusers.

Zach unfolded the orders with more curiosity than enthusiasm. Any blood he might shed in SEAL training would likely be real. There'd be blisters. And punishing endurance tests metered out to make his body stronger—physical pain to mask the raw emotional pain in a way that alcohol couldn't.

And rehab wouldn't.

Besides, he could quit drinking any time he wanted to. He just didn't want to.

Famous last words. He set down the glass of bourbon with disgust. Actions spoke volumes.

He didn't want to drink his life away.

He didn't think Michelle would want that for him, either. He felt the all-too-familiar stabs of pain.

Zach gave the paper in his hand a cursory glance, looking for the signature he knew he'd find. "Why's he doing this?"

"Maybe he thinks you deserve one more chance." Miller stalked over to the window and mercilessly drew back the curtains, letting in the blinding light of day. He threw open the sash, a cool California breeze diffusing the stench. "The family's expecting you for a late dinner tonight at the Hotel Del Coronado, 2100 sharp." Marc completed his circle of Zach's small one-room apartment. "This place stinks. Think about picking up after yourself once in a while." He stopped on his way to the door and looked Zach up and down. "A shower wouldn't hurt, either."

Put on the defensive, Zach scoffed at the suggestion, even though he intended to shower. Most days it was all he managed.

"Don't let the admiral down, Prince. Or the next time someone comes knocking at your door, it'll

be the shore patrol.'' With that parting shot, Miller
left.

Zach sank onto the mattress, all the wind
knocked out of his sails. The Chief of SEALs, Admiral Mitchell Dann, had stepped in to keep him
from going back to the brig where he'd spent the
better part of the past four weeks. And now the
man had pushed through his request for SEAL
training.

Michelle's father.

His godfather.

A man whose grief probably equaled Zach's
own, yet the admiral managed to put on a better
face for the world. How could Admiral Dann be
so forgiving of the one person who didn't deserve
it?

Zach threw the glass of bourbon. It smashed
against the wall and shattered. Shards of glass fell
to the carpet. Amber liquid rolled down the wall-
paper like the tears he wouldn't allow himself to
shed.

Moving to his dresser, he pushed aside his wallet
with the paltry sum of forty-two dollars—all that
was left of his military paycheck after drinking
most of it away. He touched his lieutenant's bars
and tried not to think.

He'd been reduced to the rank of lieutenant junior grade right after he'd punched Captain

Greene. That incident had landed him in the brig the first time. The hard drinking that followed had taken its toll, too, costing him his flight qualifications until he got his act together. Hence rehab. His one and only chance to do that.

A formal inquiry into the incident over Iraq had absolved him of any responsibility. The Navy had gone over everything with a fine-tooth comb. From cockpit banter to maintenance logs. And found nothing. In the end, top brass had determined enemy fire responsible.

He and Steve could have told them as much from their eyewitness accounts.

But he couldn't let himself off the hook that easily.

He picked up the gold wings he was no longer allowed to pin to his uniform. Closing his hand over them, he stared at the stranger in the mirror.

Miller was wrong.

Zach couldn't even muster pity for the poor bastard with the empty eyes. He shifted his gaze to the snapshot tucked into the corner of the frame, the same photo he'd once carried in the cockpit of his fighter. Now water-stained and tattered, the picture hadn't fared any better than he had.

Zach stared at it, at Michelle's achingly familiar smile. When was the last time he'd even seen her smile?

That day in the shower? In the briefing room?

Across the flight deck the corner of her mouth had turned up in a sort of sad smile. He'd wondered what she was thinking.

Now he'd never know.

As much as he blamed Greene for not letting him take that shot, he blamed himself even more. If only…

If only he'd taken it, anyway.

In one angry swoop he cleared the dresser and laid his head down. Every night Michelle called to him to come fly with her. And every morning he awoke from the nightmare of losing her all over again.

In the end he'd shot all three MiGs from the sky—except it was too late. Shooting down a hundred enemy aircraft wouldn't bring her back. Wanting to made him what kind of a dogfighter? A vengeful one?

But revenge wasn't sweet. It was bitter.

And the aftertaste made him less than a pilot. Less than a man. Less than human.

He could still feel his hand gripping the stick, his thumb poised over the trigger, his eye on the pickle. His entire life had changed course in a split second. If only he'd taken that shot, Michelle would still be alive.

He wrapped his fist tighter around his gold

wings. Felt the pin prick. Then a piercing pain.
And finally nothing.

No, that was a lie. There was so much pain bot-
tled up inside he didn't know what to do with it.

Blood oozed from between his clenched fingers,
but he barely noticed. Tears rolled from the corners
of his closed eyes. A sob escaped on a ragged
breath. Then another. Until the pain he'd tried for
so long to hold back racked his entire body. Finally
he held nothing back, and the floodgates opened,
allowing him to mourn Michelle's death for the
first time.

God, he missed her.

His best friend.

His wingman. His woman. Dead.

And he had no one to blame but himself.

Same day
SOMEWHERE IN IRAQ

MICHELLE'S HEAD POUNDED, reminding her she
was alive, which she was grateful for, at least. But
the searing pain behind her eyes made her want to
vomit. Though she didn't dare, for fear of asphyx-
iating on her own bile.

Bound and gagged, she lay on the floor of a
moving panel van in her underwear. The spaghetti-
strapped camisole and matching cotton underpants

that had been white when she'd left ship were now a less discriminating color. Her bra had disappeared along with the rest of her gear.

She didn't know which was worse, the way she smelled or the way she looked. Not that it mattered.

After ejecting from the cockpit, bruised and battered as she was from the explosive force of twelve thousand pounds of thrust, she'd still fared better than her RIO. Closing her eyes against the all too vivid memory, Michelle offered up a silent prayer for Skeeter.

Alone, with nothing but her survival vest, Michelle had managed to evade capture for four days in the mountains of northern Iraq, where her plane had drilled a burning hole into the ground. Even when she'd realized her beacon wasn't working and rescue wasn't imminent, she hadn't given up hope.

Zach knew where she was. He'd find her.

But he hadn't.

And she'd been captured.

She didn't know if it had been weeks or even months from the day she'd been shot down.

Had he fared any better?

She'd left him outnumbered and outgunned three to one. He was good, maybe, as far as F-14 pilots went, the best, but the odds were against him.

She missed him with an ache so deep it left her empty.

She'd let him down. She'd let Skeeter down. She'd let herself down....

Her father. Her country. The list was endless.

There were no points for second place. Just one of the fighter pilot's credo. For once she wasn't jealous of always being second best to Zach Prince. It gave her hope that he'd pulled off the impossible.

Something she'd been unable to do.

Since she'd been taken prisoner, day passed into one long nightmare without end, making it hard to care about anything. She tried to push the self-defeating thoughts aside and remind herself she had a family who loved her.

All she had to do was survive.

She didn't know anymore if she had the strength to make it through this. Or for another escape attempt. This time they'd caught her trying to break out a boarded window in her prison. So they were moving her again in their overheated van.

Zach's sister, Tabby, had once shown her how Navy SEALs learned to swim with their hands and feet bound. If there was any way out of here, she'd willingly swim all the way back to the ship.

The ship. Zach.

Please don't be dead....

She didn't know how she'd go on living if he was.

The steady motion and oppressive heat had her drifting in and out of consciousness, where she dreamed of ships and planes. And of a hotshot pilot who made it though the flames of hell just to reach her.

THE NEXT TIME Michelle came to, her mobile world had come to a standstill. In fact, she didn't think she was even in the van anymore. Awareness of her new surroundings came in slow degrees as she blinked open her eyes.

She looked around the dark cell. A basement, judging from the small, high grimy window with its wrought-iron bars.

From the dampness beneath her cheek she suspected she lay in a pool of blood coming from the gash on her forehead. Couldn't they come up with a better knockout drug than hitting her over the head every time they wanted to relocate her? At least the headache was gone.

Lying there, she listened to the sound of rats and roaches scurrying about, glad the corners of the room were too dark for her to see the creatures that kept her company.

With a great deal of effort, Michelle pushed herself into a sitting position and leaned back against the cinder-block wall. Her hands tingled as blood circulated back into the restricted appendages. She pulled at the restraints, testing the bonds securing her wrists and ankles, but they held fast.

The basement door creaked open.

Her heart skipped a beat. Instinctively she drew her knees toward her body and hunched her shoulders.

Ali, the fat one she called Ollie, stood in the doorway. She avoided eye contact as he stepped into the small cell and began shouting at her in Arabic. He waved his arms impatiently when she didn't respond. Knocking her onto her side, he planted one booted foot on her matted hair. As Michelle struggled to free herself, Ali motioned to Ihassan, his nervous sidekick, to cut her bonds. She called him Stan.

Only then did Ollie remove his boot from her hair. She sat up, rubbing her unbound wrists. Then freed herself of the rope at her ankles and the gag in her mouth. "Bastard," she croaked out between parched lips.

That bit of defiance earned her a slap that started her ears ringing. Cradling her cheek, she stared daggers at Ollie.

As captors, Stan and Ollie were as inept as the

comedic duo she'd named them after. If it wasn't for the automatic weapons that gave them a distinct advantage, at least one of her escape attempts would have been successful.

She suspected they moved her so often because they didn't know what to do with her. That, and because, for some unexplained reason, she made them nervous.

Ollie wrenched her arm. Pointing at the Norplant just beneath her skin, he argued with Stan. They'd discovered the implant in their initial strip search, and from what she gathered, they thought her birth control was some kind of tracking or explosive device forced on her by the Devil President of the United States.

After the lengthy argument, Stan disappeared, then reappeared with a bundle she recognized as the drab olive green of her confiscated flight suit. He threw it on the ground in the front of her. Then the two men left her alone.

As soon as she heard the key turn in the lock, Michelle reached for her uniform. She picked up the bloodstained cloth and hugged it to her. Even though her survival vest and equipment were still missing, this was something. Her heart beat so fast she felt as if it would implode.

Unbound. Uniform.

They'd decided what to do with her.

Michelle scrambled to her feet only to find her legs couldn't support her. Her hand touched solid bedrock where the cinder blocks had crumbled away. She wouldn't be digging her way out of this prison. But where there was a will there was a way.

And she had to find that will.

Michelle used the wall to steady herself. She shook out her jumper with its red, white and blue flag and various other patches signifying her ship and her squadron.

Gingerly stepping into the flight suit, she zipped it up only to realize the outfit dwarfed her. For reassurance, she touched her identifying leather wings. Still hers. She knew she'd lost weight. She just hadn't realized how much.

Her bare toes curled into the dirt floor. Aside from the lack of food and relatively poor treatment, they hadn't seriously harmed her. At least it wasn't as bad as it could have been. It was the uncertainty, not knowing, like now, that tortured her.

When it became obvious Stan and Ollie weren't coming back anytime soon, Michelle sank down to the dirt again. She patted down her pockets, looking for what, she didn't know. Something useful they hadn't taken. A pencil. A piece of paper. A loaded gun.

A memory flashed.

Preflight briefing. Zach winking at her from across the aisle.

She dug into the cargo pocket of her left leg where she found lint—and one squashed piece of Bazooka bubble gum.

She put a hand to her mouth to keep the hysterical laughter from bubbling up. "Oh, Zach," she murmured. "I could really use a good joke right about now."

She wiped away a sniffle as she unwrapped her gift. There wasn't much light, so she scooted over to the beam from the single window, all the while keeping a wary eye on the door.

What she found made her choke back a sob.

Zach had erased the joke and penned the words *Marry me* inside the little cartoon balloon. Pressed into the gum was a small gold band with an equally unassuming diamond. So unlike Zach. But just her style. Of course, it could be cubic zirconium for all she knew.

She blinked back the salty tears. She hadn't cried once since her capture. And now she was about to fall apart over a ring that could simply be the man's worst joke to date.

In the interests of her very survival, she pushed aside thoughts of Zach. She didn't know if he was alive or dead.

Or hurting. And needing her.

Like she needed him now.

I don't love you! I've never loved you.

Why can't you just leave me alone?

"Please, don't let that be my last face-to-face words with him," she prayed. "I do love you, Zach. I've always loved you. And I'm scared here all alone."

Michelle closed her eyes against the flood of tears that threatened to overwhelm her. "I can't fall apart now. I can't."

Oh, God, she was talking to herself.

She sucked up a ragged breath, then concentrated on her discovery. Bits and pieces of pink goo stuck to the band as she freed it. She put every last bit of gum in her mouth, relishing the sugar rush.

She turned the sticky ring over in her palm. It looked real enough. So if it wasn't a joke, what was it?

A proposal.

It was what she'd wanted and waited for all her life. And feared. And he was dead. And she was never getting out of this hellhole. So what did it matter, anyway?

It mattered, it mattered, her heart cried.

She started to put it on the ring finger of her left hand, then thought better of the idea. Instead, she hid the ring in her mouth for safekeeping.

She jumped as the door opened again. Ollie entered her cell with his usual flurry. Grabbing her by her collar, he yanked her to her feet. Once more, he tied her hands behind her back, then forced her into the outer room.

Her prized possession went undetected tucked in her cheek. She prayed she wouldn't be forced to make another videotaped confession right now.

She'd read a prepared statement to the camera after she'd first been captured, careful to pronounce each word exactly as written, hoping the bad diction would clue in the viewer. Hoping someone would see it. Hoping they wouldn't believe for a minute that the words denouncing her country and Commander in Chief came from her.

Stan joined them, holding her survival vest in one hand and waving what she recognized as her 9-mm pistol in the other. He aimed it at her chest and she stumbled backward into Ollie, who forced her to her knees.

Stan and Ollie argued over her head. She may not know the language, but their intent translated clearly enough.

They were going to kill her.

They were just fighting over the honor.

She couldn't die like this. Bile rose in her throat. She choked it down. The ring triggered her gag reflex. She coughed. Keeping her mouth closed, she tried, between spurts of coughing, to keep her precious treasure hidden.

Michelle attempted to swallow the ring. But the butt end of Ollie's automatic weapon slammed between her shoulder blades before she got the chance.

Zach's ring flew from her mouth.

It rolled silently across the dirt floor and stopped at Stan's sandal-clad feet. Her world spun in slow motion as the skinny man bent to pick it up.

She held her breath, unwilling to betray her emotions. Not for the first time she wished she had Tabby's training and her father's experience as a Navy SEAL. They would know what to do in this situation.

But they weren't in this situation. She was.

Her gaze zeroed in on the man standing before her. He ignored her to examine the gold, biting the soft metal to test its authenticity. Michelle picked frantically at the knots binding her hands, hoping Ollie's focus was equally intent on the ring.

Stan jabbered something to Ollie. Waving the pistol, the skinny man invoked their leader's name. Michelle had pieced together the fact that they were deserters from the Republican Guard, but she couldn't figure out how or if they fit into the rebel cause. Or why they'd hold her for so long just to shoot her in the end.

Should she try to barter her freedom with Zach's ring? She didn't want to part with it. But they already had it. And they'd already helped themselves to everything else that was once hers. At the moment she didn't have anything to lose by trying. Any maybe her life if she didn't.

"Let me go and you can keep the ring. Me go. You keep." Did she actually think she could bridge the language barrier with Tarzaneeze? She may as well be speaking pig Latin.

Stan laughed at something Ollie said. She dared a look over her shoulder. A wide grin spread across Ollie's porky face as he met her gaze, and both men started laughing.

"You keep," Stan repeated in his tinny voice, pocketing the gold band.

"I'm glad you think it's so funny," she snapped as Zach's ring disappeared. And with it her hope. If only she had her pointee-talkee.

Yes! Her pointee-talkee.

The aid had been in one of the pockets of her survival vest. But they'd stripped her of everything before she'd gotten the chance to use it. Did she dare hope it was still there? With her bound hands, she tried to point frantically at the vest in Stan's hand.

She nodded her encouragement as the fellow rummaged through the pockets. Dog tags dropped to the dirt, along with her compass and a growing pile of other useful items. Finally he found the communication aid and a piece of material called a blood chit. Michelle almost wept with relief when he tossed the vest aside and waved the two items at her.

"Yes, yes!" The pointee-talkee listed selected phrases in English opposite the Arabic translation. The blood chit depicted an American flag and promised great rewards to anyone assisting the bearer to safety.

"Lies!" Stan wadded the blood chit and stuffed it into his pocket along with the ring.

Well, the man spoke one English word clearly enough.

"No, not lies!"

Stan and Ollie started arguing again. When did they ever stop?

Inside she begged for her life. Outside she wouldn't allow the facade to crack and continued to work at unraveling the rope binding her hands behind her back. Somehow she had to free herself, disarm two men and escape Iraq on foot. Or convince them she spoke the truth and enlist their help. "Not lies," she repeated.

Both tasks seemed equally daunting. But her only other option was to die trying.

They were no longer even listening as they argued over her ring. She kept her eyes on Stan. And read Ollie through the other man's reactions. As long as the nervous-looking fellow had the gun she might stand a chance. He'd never once raised a hand to her. Could she convince him the evasion aids were telling the truth?

Despite her promises he soon gave in to the fat bully's overt demands. All hope fled as he handed Ollie the gun.

Michelle felt the touch of cold steel as Ollie put the muzzle of her own pistol to the back of her head, execution-style.

No! her mind rebelled. *I will not die like this.*

She heard the click as he chambered a round.

CHAPTER FOUR

ZACH SPOTTED his family right away, the big noisy group in the corner of the outdoor piazza with its firefly lights twinkling against the backdrop of a moonless night.

Varsity night, pilots called it.

A moonless night at sea made for rough landing conditions. And the experienced pilots knew it. The less experienced soon learned it. When Commanders filled out the duty rosters, they snagged all the full moons for themselves. The lower the rank, the darker the night.

A night prone to accidents.

A dangerous night.

A shiver raced down his spine. Goose bumps peppered his flesh.

The naval aviator in him put a name to the feel-

ing he hadn't been able to shake all evening—
dread.

Something was in the air tonight.

Zach put his sunglasses back on. As unnecessary
as they were this late in the evening, he still needed
them to shield his emotions. He'd made a mistake
in coming here. He turned to leave, but it was too
late.

"Zach," the family chorus greeted him.

He could barely stand to face them all: mother,
father, sister, brother-in-law, baby niece and
adopted nephew.

But he stowed his reservations and turned back
around.

"Join us." His father—Captain Tad Prince, retired—commanded, hailing a nearby waiter.

"We just started in on the salad." His mother
smiled up at him.

"Sit by me, Uncle Zach," seven-year-old Aaron
invited.

"Sure thing, sport." Zach forced the upbeat
tone, even managed to ruffle the boy's dark hair.
It all seemed so normal. Yet there was nothing
"normal" about the way he felt.

His brother-in-law offered his chair and pulled
up another from a nearby table, quite a change
from the hard-ass who'd knocked on his door that
morning.

Tonight they were just family.

In fact, Marc didn't even mention that Zach was twenty minutes late. Twenty minutes Zach had spent at the Officers' Club in Miramar deciding if he would have another drink or be a man and face his family.

"What's with the shades?" his father asked as Zach took his seat.

Zach hesitated only a moment before removing his aviator sunglasses and hooking them onto the pocket of his bomber jacket. He knew an order from his old man when he heard one.

He heard his mother suck in her breath. The rest were a little more subtle in their reactions. There was one unspoken question on everyone's lips: Was he even sober? He didn't give a damn what they thought of his bloodshot eyes as long as they didn't guess the truth.

The waiter materialized. "Another round," his dad ordered. "And a beer with a whiskey chaser for my boy here." He patted Zach on the back. His old man subscribed to the hair-of-the-dog theory.

"Very good, sir," the uniformed server responded.

Zach cocked a wry grin in his father's direction. "Make that a diet root beer," he corrected, absently running a hand over his flat stomach. He made a quick selection from the menu before the waiter had a chance to disappear.

He didn't have to buy into his dad's methodology as an adult. But he got the feeling his parents were glad he wasn't having a drink. They exchanged a parental smile. And his mother reached out and caressed the scar bracketing the right side of his father's face. They'd always been a touchy-feely couple. It had embarrassed Zach as a kid. Now it simply amazed him. They'd somehow managed to keep their marriage strong even through years of hardship and separation while his frogman father had been deployed on one mission after another with the SEALs.

"Son, we're glad you decided to join us tonight," his father stated simply.

"Now, if only Bowie were here," his mother added. Lily Prince lived for the moments the family got together and she could take snapshots to commemorate those increasingly rare occasions.

There was general agreement. Everyone missed Bowie. Zach felt a twinge of guilt. He'd avoided his younger brother's calls all month, effectively shutting out the one person who might have understood what he was going through. "Where is the little squirt these days?"

"Guam," his father answered, toying with his beer bottle. Tad Prince never sat still for very long.

And never without fidgeting. "He's traveling the South Pacific. Damn shame his eyesight keeps him out of the SEAL program."

"Bowie loves his job as a SeaBee, Dad," Tabby said, punctuating her words with her salad fork. "Besides, you already have me following in your footsteps and now Zach."

His dad warmed to the subject. "Did you know your sister will be one of your SEAL instructors?"

"No joke?" He *was* in hell.

"Tabitha's coming on board to prepare for the first class of female trainees later this year." Marc's eyes lit up when he looked at his wife. The pair practically lived in their uniforms, so they were never publicly affectionate. But the smoldering looks made a guy wonder if they were going to drop to the tile patio and go at it right there.

Get a room.

"Marc's accepted the position as Commander Naval Special Warfare." Tabby beamed with pride. "Brad Bailey from Team One is moving into the SEAL Commanding Officer of Training position."

Could he and Michelle have managed dual military careers like that? And kids? Lots of kids.

God, he felt so alone.

Their waiter arrived with his salad and soft drink. "Your soda, sir." The man set the salad and drink in front of him, then moved around the table with a round of beers and kiddie cocktails. It was on the tip of Zach's tongue to tell the server to take the soda back and bring him something stronger, when the color caught the light.

His waning smile turned nostalgic. Michelle had eyes that exact color, root beer. Funny how he could remember them so clearly. Just like the smoking incident from their childhood.

At age eleven he'd taken one of his dad's Cuban cigars, wanting to see what all the fuss was about. Michelle had offered her usual protest when he'd shown it to her, so he'd traded the fancy gold-foil cigar band for her promise to stay. And they'd lit up out behind the Danns' barn. He'd taken a couple puffs of the nasty thing just to show off. Convinced Michelle to try it and grossed her out. Then took a couple more puffs to prove himself.

His dad had caught them. Zach had almost started a fire trying to put the thing out. Michelle had been sent home to tattle on herself, and Goody Two-shoes that she was, she did. His dad had lit up another cigar and invited Zach to finish his, talking to him as if he were an adult, conversely reminding him he was still a kid. But the cigar had lost all appeal. And that evening out behind the Danns' barn, Zach had buried his desire to smoke, along with the contents of his stomach.

Oh, to be a kid again.

Dinner arrived and throughout the main course Aaron entertained him with a story about a home run he'd hit over the fence, almost.

This was exactly what Zach needed right now.

He'd been trying to go it alone for so long he'd forgotten how much family meant to him.

"It would have gone way over the fence," Aaron insisted. "But the wind dropped it."

"That so?" Zach listened to his nephew with interest and encouraged the boy to keep right on talking. It beat the hell out of listening to his own thoughts. Aaron finished the baseball tale and started in on another. The boy had a very active imagination.

Not to be outdone by her big brother, Mariah began to fuss. Zach insisted on holding his niece so his sister could finish her meal.

While his dinner sat untouched, the "little miracle" rested her sleepy head against his chest, making him feel big and awkward. He patted her back and was rewarded with an unladylike belch. Soon afterward her eyes drifted closed.

Holding the baby while she slept stirred something deep within his lost soul. Something that made his heart ache just a little bit more.

A little bit of heaven on earth that he'd lost.

Smoothing his hand over the baby's silky cap of

dark hair, Zach stopped to fix a slipping pink bow. Who dressed her like that, anyway? Not his sister, must be Marc.

Zach exchanged a knowing glance with his brother-in-law, but didn't come right out and accuse the man of sending subliminal messages to his own daughter. Somehow Zach knew that the bond between father and daughter was a special one, which even Tabby with her gender-neutral mothering would have a hard time usurping. *Chalk one up for our side.*

"Do me a favor, kiddo," Zach whispered into her shell-like ear for reinforcement. "Don't grow up to be a warrior woman. Bring guys to their knees the old-fashioned way. With apple pie."

"I heard that, little brother," Tabby chided. "If you're going to fill my daughter's head with nonsense, I'll take her now, please."

"What'd I say?" Zach reluctantly handed back the baby.

"We're *all* going to encourage Mariah and Aaron to follow their hearts," she lectured. "To be all that they can be."

She sounded like a poster girl for love, peace and happiness. Not to mention the Army. Too bad life didn't always work out that way. He'd followed his heart all right. But no one ever warned him it could be cut right out of a living, breathing body. And die, along with his dreams.

"I'm gonna be a baseball player when I grow up," Aaron said, demanding his attention. "Or maybe a garbage man." The adults at the table smiled at the seriousness of his declaration, but weren't surprised by another career change in the very next breath. "Or maybe a pilot like you, Uncle Zach. Can you take me up in your plane this weekend?"

Zach turned his plate clockwise a fraction and placed his napkin in his lap, pretending sudden interest in his food. He'd taken Aaron for rides before. Even though the Navy had grounded him, he still had his private pilot's license. He kept a single-engine Cessna Skyhawk at a private airfield near the base.

But he hadn't flown since the crash.

He needed more time.

He missed flying. Maybe almost as much as he missed Michelle. He just hadn't realized how much until his nephew put it into words.

But flying solo held little appeal.

He certainly wasn't in any condition to give his nephew a ride. "Not this weekend, sport. But some weekend real soon."

His mother wasn't about to let the subject drop, however. "Why not this Sunday? You won't get another chance before you start SEAL training. You could take your dad and me and Aaron up. We'll make a day of it.''

"Mom…" He tried to come up with a plausible excuse. He wasn't even fit to drive his car, let alone fly his plane. "It's been a while.''

"We don't want to see you give up your dream of flying, Zach," his mother said.

Ouch. Rip off that bandage, Mom. What happened to mothers who kissed your boo-boos and made them go away?

"Well, if you're not up to it…"

Leave it to his father to push him off the deep end with a challenge once he realized he might be ready for the wading pool.

Zach had detected the slightest hint of reproach in his father's voice. And that was all the old man had to say. Before Zach knew what he was doing, he'd agreed to take his parents and Aaron flying on Sunday. "All right.''

"Good, Sunday it is. Now, who's ready for dessert?" his dad asked.

"I left my camera in the room. I'll just go get it and be right back." His mother placed her napkin on the table.

"Don't get up, Mom. Finish your dinner. I'll get it for you," Zach offered. "Aaron can come with me.''

She handed over the room key. Zach, with his nephew in tow, went to retrieve it. They found the digital camera easily enough, right on top of her suitcase where she said it would be. And returned within a matter of minutes.

The table fell silent as they approached.

He'd been set up.

A small cake had replaced his dinner plate. Two large candles, shaped like a three and a zero, burned brightly in the center. A couple of presents had appeared, as well.

"Happy birthday, Uncle Zach!" Aaron beamed up at him.

"We thought since you'd be in SEAL training next week, we'd just go ahead and celebrate tonight," his mother explained.

He hadn't even bothered to ask if Marc's promotion or something else had brought his parents to California this time. He was used to their frequent jaunts. When Zach was about nine, his father had retired from the Navy and the family had settled in Key West where his mother's salvage operation was based. Lily Chapel Prince had spent the years before she married treasure troving and had returned to it later—the only difference now was that the family business was as much a hobby as photography.

Next to him Aaron bounced up and down, barely

able to contain his excitement. "Here's your camera, Grandma. I did good. I didn't even tell."

"You did great!" Lily Prince congratulated her grandson.

She meant well. They all did. But Zach would have preferred thirty to come and go without his notice.

He wouldn't spoil it for them, though.

"Thank you." He gripped the back of his chair. A strained smile spread across his face. "You really shouldn't have gone to all this trouble."

He meant it.

"We got you a hat, Uncle Zach." Aaron climbed up on Zach's chair to put the Navy SEAL ball cap on his head. He giggled when Zach turned it backward.

"I need to be able to sight down the barrel of my firearm."

"And Grandpa got you this." Aaron held out a small hinged box decorated in navy blue and gold. The kind military awards came in.

And Zach knew his father's gift.

He swallowed back the lump in his throat and flipped it open to find his old man's Navy SEAL Trident. An eagle grasping Neptune's pitchfork in one claw and a weapon in the other.

"I just happened to have an old Budweiser lying around." He used the SEAL's nickname for the pin, meaning wiser than BUD/S, the term for a trainee. "And since you're headed off to SEAL training—" his dad cleared his throat "—well, I just thought it would be incentive. Or good luck or something…"

The weight of those words came down hard on Zach's shoulders. No room for failure.

But wasn't he going into SEAL training only because he'd already failed as a pilot? He'd failed to protect his wingman. And Michelle and Skeeter had paid with their lives.

"Smile, everyone." *Click.*

"Time's running out on those candles," Marc pointed out.

Zach forced his attention back to the birthday cake. Wax from the numbers dripped onto the frosting. But all he could do was stare at the flame. He'd almost been able to distract himself. Almost.

He looked up at the moonless sky. A chill raced down his spine. Cold sweat beaded his forehead. The ringing in his ears drowned out the background noise until the only sound was the unsteady rhythm of his own heart.

"Zach," his mother queried. "Honey, what's wrong?"

"We always celebrated together."

Michelle's birthday was six days before his.

Today.

"Oh, Zach. I'm so sorry. How thoughtless of me." His mother expressed genuine distress. And Zach wanted to put her at ease, but couldn't find the energy to fake it anymore. If there'd been a moon, he'd have thrown back his head and howled his agony.

"Make a wish, Uncle Zach," Aaron pleaded in the soft whisper of a child who sensed tension in the air and wanted to diminish it. Marc squeezed the boy's hand in a silent signal that only father and son understood.

If only wishing could make it so.

If only...

"What birthday was it," Zach began, "when Michelle had the Barbie birthday cake?"

"Fifth," his mother supplied solemnly.

"I yanked out the doll before she even got to blow out the candles." Michelle had cried so hard. "And the next year I just went ahead and blew out her candles." She'd cried then, too. "And there was the year I smashed the piñata before she even got to take a swing.

"I'd just like to know if anyone remembers a birthday when I didn't make her cry."

Life had been so simple back then. A smashed piñata had seemed funny at the time. And when you messed up, you called for *"do overs."* He scanned the somber faces of his family.

This year was supposed to be different. He'd plotted to wine and dine her while they planned their future. But he hadn't even been able to wait to give her the ring....

His whole life he'd played the clown. He'd even wrapped that cheap ring in a comic strip. How corny.

Whatever made him think he could make her happy?

"I didn't think so." The lone surviving candle burned down to the quick, flickered and went out. "I wish for do overs." His voice cracked. He kept his eyes downcast rather than face the pitying stares of his family.

"Do you need a hug, Uncle Zach?"

Zach's gaze locked on to Aaron's. Thirty-year-old men didn't need hugs. His eyes and his throat burned. So he just nodded. His nephew wrapped him in a big bear hug. The next thing he knew, his mother propelled herself into his arms. And Tabby, holding Mariah, launched herself at him from the other direction.

Adults didn't get second chances. There were no points for second place in naval aviation. And in the SEALs the only easy day was yesterday.

And all his yesterdays were gone.

His tomorrows weren't looking too bright, either.

But tonight he had his family.

His dad's cell phone rang, interrupting their group hug.

"Tad, don't answer it," his mother scolded, wiping tears from her eyes.

"It could be Bowie," he said, moving away from the table and toward the terrace rail to engage in quiet conversation. Obviously the caller was not the youngest Prince son, or the phone would have been passed around.

"I hate these modern inconveniences," his mother fussed. "You should see him with e-mail and instant messages. I swear he logs on every hour. He has friends around the globe. At least I don't think he's having cyber sex or checking out cyber porn."

On that note his mother ended the embrace, and the women took their seats. Aaron hopped down from his chair. Zach remained standing and used the opportunity to take his leave. "I hope everyone will understand if I excuse myself from the party."

Before he got the chance, however, his old man returned with a mostly unreadable expression on his weathered face. "That was the Chief of SEALs," he announced. "Team One has recovered the body of a female pilot."

Dead silence hung over the table.

Zach felt the pull of twelve G's. All the air

rushed from his lungs. He couldn't breathe. And at the same time he wanted to explode.

"The casket is due to arrive in D.C. tomorrow morning," his dad continued before anyone could even catch their breath. "Mitch has to ID the body. He wants me there."

"I'll go pack." His mother got up to leave the table.

"I'm going, too." Zach forced himself to stay on his feet.

0734 Saturday
NAVAL HOSPITAL,
Bethesda, MD

ZACH HEARD the general hum and buzz of the hospital and the conversations going on around him as if from a great distance. He focused on the four most important people in his life right now, all walking ahead of him. His parents and Michelle's.

The rest of the sterile world passed by in slow motion. With the single exception of their escort, a young coroner. The lieutenant wore no rank on his green scrubs, but had introduced himself upon their arrival at the Bethesda Naval Hospital a few minutes earlier.

Zach had managed little more than a fitful nap in the admiral's private jet. His father, a retired captain, wore his khaki uniform. As did Zach. The polyester knit traveled better than he did, so at least he didn't think he looked as wrung out as he felt.

He wasn't up to the task that lay ahead.

Since their arrival, Zach had avoided direct contact with the Danns. With his parents around that was easy enough.

Maybe the Danns didn't blame him.

But he blamed himself.

He felt awkward with Michelle's parents now and didn't imagine it would get easier. He just wished it didn't have to be this way. There was so much he wanted to say to his godparents. Beginning with, "I'm sorry."

Admiral Dann had dressed up for the somber occasion, an intimidating picture in his "choker whites" with all that gold braid and row upon row of service ribbons. Few would even notice how heavily he leaned on his walking stick. Zach noticed.

They reached the morgue and the coroner began cataloging the injuries. "The body's remarkably well preserved, considering," he explained. "Female, mid-to late-twenties. Severe trauma. Burns over twenty-five percent..."

Zach couldn't bear to hear another word. Michelle wasn't just another toe-tagged corpse in a body bag. To him she was far more than the sum of her injuries and always would be. He stopped at a beverage vending machine and fed it quarters in an effort to regain his bearing. He punched the button for coffee, black. But the damn cup didn't come down. And the coffee poured through the drain.

As inappropriate as it was, he almost laughed out loud. What fickle finger of fate had brought him to this point in time? *God, he missed her.*

Resting his arm atop the machine and his forehead against it, he turned his head and stared down the passageway. His father and the admiral entered the viewing room with the doctor. He could see them through the open curtains of the framed window. A blue bark, or coffin escort, had traveled with the deceased body from the Middle East and stood at parade rest beside the door. His mother and Michelle's had remained outside.

"I can't go in there," Augusta Dann said in her soft German accent. "I can't." With trembling hands she clutched the royal-blue teddy bear Zach had won for Michelle years ago when they'd gone to see the Blue Angels' air show at the base.

Augusta Dann looked small and vulnerable even though she towered over his own mother, who began to croon soothingly to her. In fact, from this distance, Augusta looked just the way Michelle had after he'd spent twenty bucks exercising his pitching arm to win her that stuffed animal.

Michelle had clutched it to her as if it was the most precious thing in the world. And she'd looked at him as if he'd managed the impossible.

"Look, his fur matches your eyes." She'd held the furry toy up next to his face.

"How'd you know it's a he? Did you check?" Zach snagged the bear from her and checked its underbelly. He got a kick out of holding it out of her reach when she tried to get it back. What she didn't realize was how much all that wrestling for the bear turned him on.

"Zach, you perv." She finally managed to grab the bear from him.

"I'm not a pervert." Just seventeen. And horny. "Hey. A minute ago you were all over me with gratitude."

She toyed with the bear's goggles and silk scarf. "Well, that was before you opened your big mouth. Maybe you should just keep it shut for a change."

He pretended to zip his mouth closed.

"There's your brother and sister. They're probably looking for us." Michelle waved to his siblings. "Tabby, Bowie—"

Zach dragged her behind the row of tented game booths along the open-air arcade.

"Zach—" she protested.

"Shh. I don't want them to see us."

"Well, why not?"

He stood there looking down at her. Her back pressed against the striped canvas. His body pressed against hers. He didn't really have a reason. And all he could think of to say was "Because…"

Zach leaned in and kissed her, a tentative touch of his lips to hers. After several skipped heartbeats he pulled back to look into her eyes.

Soft and round.

Like her young body. Her breasts rose and fell against his chest. He could hear her breathing, feel it fan his face and mingle with his own.

"I don't think I'm going to be able to keep my mouth shut," he said, and leaned in again just as she opened hers to object. He sealed her protest, letting his tongue explore.

She wrapped her arms around his neck, bear dangling from her hand. Her body melded to his, all soft curves pressed against hard angles. Then her tongue touched his, and the ache in his groin became exquisite torture.

He wanted to go on kissing her this way forever.

Finally he either had to come up for air or quit breathing altogether. He chose oxygen. And got a good look at her flushed face.

He cocked a grin.

"Michelle Dann. Was that your first French kiss?" he teased.

She blushed a deep shade of crimson, and her eyes searched his. "Was I your...?"

She couldn't even say it. She was the geek. And he was the jock about to start his senior year of high school. As an All-Varsity Junior, he'd lettered in three sports the previous school year. Cheerleaders with perky breasts worshiped him. Girls of all shapes and sizes wanted him.

And he didn't know how to tell her that a make-out session with anyone else wouldn't mean as much as one of their late-night chats, no matter what the subject, physics or poetry. Because she lived in Virginia and he lived in Florida, most of those conversations took place on the phone.

Except in the summer. When their families got together and he could spend time with her.

So he did what any self-respecting seventeen-year-old boy would do. "No," he lied. "I've kissed lots of girls."

She pushed away from the tent canvas, looking suddenly vulnerable as she wrapped her arms around that bear, instead of him....

"Smooth move, hotshot," Zach pounded his fist against the hospital vending machine.

"Oh, that machine does that all the time," a

hospital corpsman said in passing. "There's coffee in the cafeteria."

Zach's head whipped up. He snorted a laugh, the sound releasing his mounting tension. Then he instantly sobered. Because there was nothing funny about this situation.

He looked down that long stretch of corridor.

I can't. I can't.

Mrs. Dann's words echoed in his head.

But at last he mustered the courage to move down the hall. He knew what he had to do.

And that was see Michelle just one last time.

The marine posted by the door snapped to attention. Zach passed the escort, gathering all his reserves in one breath before entering the viewing room.

The cold caught him off guard. And the smells. Of antiseptic mingled with the stench of rotting flesh.

He brought up a hand to cover his nose and mouth.

The coroner hovered over the draped body. His father and the admiral stood off to the side.

"I don't want to see her this way," Admiral Dann admitted, shaking his head. "God, I hadn't even seen my own daughter in a year. The last time I talked to her it was to lecture."

The strain in the admiral's voice was hard to

take. In his entire life Zach had never seen the man fall apart. Without a word to the others in the room Zach walked over to the gurney and reached for the green sheet draping the body.

The coroner offered him a surgical mask. "I should warn you, the face is an exit wound for a hollow-point bullet. It's not a pretty sight."

"Bullet?" Zach repeated. "Not an explosion?" The punch to the gut feeling left him reeling.

"Point blank," the coroner started by answering his first question. "Self-inflicted, maybe, judging from the powder burns to her hands, though she could also have struggled with her executioner. We're going to have a tough time matching what remain of the teeth with dental records."

The doctor went on to explain his observations.

But Zach had heard enough. He pulled back the drape to see for himself. Holding his breath, he counted the beats of his heart. One, one thousand. Two, two thousand.

His gaze swept the faceless corpse from singed brown hair to toe tag. Her skin was gray, pasty, and mottled by bruised and burned flesh.

Cold to the touch, he noted, stroking her arm. He couldn't begin to describe the feeling of relief.

"Skeeter Daniels. Lieutenant Junior Grade Sara Daniels," Zach said. And the last time he'd seen her, those small breasts had been cupped in ivory lace. "Michelle's RIO. She's from Newport, Virginia. Both her parents and her kid brother still live there. I think."

He stared at the body a moment longer, trying to reconcile the corpse with the way he remembered her. She'd earned the tag Skeeter shooting skeet with her father. At target practice, she could outgun any sailor on board the *Enterprise* and a few marines to boot.

All the bits and pieces Michelle had shared with him about Skeeter over the months during their deployment fell into place. But he'd never really taken the time to know Sara, and now he'd never get the chance.

Guilt warred with relief. This body wasn't Michelle's. But Skeeter never should have died under his command. And she had family who would mourn her passing.

"The bruises?" he asked. They looked similar to ones he'd recently suffered.

"Ejection harness," the coroner replied, confirming his suspicions. "Broken back. Severe internal injuries. A severed spinal cord."

A loose or improperly fit cinch.

Eject! Eject, dammit!

Zach hadn't seen much of anything except red after the tail of Michelle's plane burst into flames. They'd heard the sonic boom when the jet hit the mountain, saw the flames. And kept a lookout for the chutes…

"Tell me they ejected!" he'd demanded of his RIO, willing his words to make it happen. His head snapped from one direction to another, trying to angle for a better look. "Tower, we're engaged! Tomcat down. Repeat, Tomcat Two down."

"Get your ass out of there, hotshot."

"No chutes!" Steve confirmed the worst.

"Dammit! Keep looking."

"We've got MiGs at two and six o'clock." Steve worked diligently as his extra pair of eyes.

"No can do, Tower. I'm going after these guys." The MiGs whizzed passed in a game of chicken Zach had no intention of losing. He turned the plane in a split S and went in pursuit.

"That's an order, Renegade."

"Backup?" he asked Steve.

"ETA, two minutes on those Hornets."

"Screw the Hornets. And screw the captain's orders…."

He'd paid for that decision. And all the ones that followed. But until now he hadn't realized the true price. He'd missed eyeballing the chutes.

Skeeter was dead.

But what about Michelle? It only took one pull of the cord to jettison them both. Either Skeeter had pulled that cord, or Michelle had. Skeeter's injuries were evidence of what could go wrong during an emergency ejection. Zach chose to focus on what could go right.

Lieutenant Dann's official classification—missing in action, presumed dead—suddenly took on new meaning.

Presumed was a hell of a word.

Hope mingled with gut-wrenching fear.

Alive or dead, she was somewhere in Iraq.

Lost in mind-numbing self-pity, he'd wasted too much time already.

Holding the mask to his nose and mouth, he looked up and met the admiral's gaze from across the room. Both his father and godfather had strange expressions on their faces. As if seeing for the first time what had been there all along.

He and Michelle had been lovers.

Albeit young lovers. And only that one time…

"I'm going after her," Zach announced. He turned and left the viewing room.

"Zach!" Admiral Dann called him back.

Zach spun on his heel to face a man who right now looked every one of his sixty-some years.

"You go off half-cocked and you'll get yourself killed! For the past month my teams have been scouring the Middle East for some shred of evidence that these two were still alive. They found a grave. They found a body. Sara Daniels is dead.

I want to believe Michelle is alive as much as you do. I'm not going to give up on my own flesh and blood.''

"They ejected from the plane, Mitch! That's all the evidence *I* need. Michelle is my wingman. My responsibility. And somehow I forgot the most important credo of naval aviation. *Never* leave your wingman.''

"Son.'' His dad jumped headlong into the emotionally charged shouting match. "You were outnumbered. Do you think anyone here blames you for not seeing those chutes?''

"I don't know. Ask Michelle. *Ask Sara.*''

Closing his eyes against the pain, Zach turned from his father and godfather. He plowed a hand through his short military cut and counted to ten before opening his eyes again. "I'm not going to wait another day for *someone* to bring her home in a body bag. If she's out there, alive or dead, I'll find her and bring her back myself. That's not a promise, that's a fact.''

He met and held his godfather's gaze, felt his father and the coroner looking at him with pity, felt the burning behind his eyes.

Big boys didn't cry.

They didn't make little girls cry, either. And they sure as hell didn't leave them to die alone.

Zach stormed from the room.

His mother and Mrs. Dann looked up expectantly. Both his father and the admiral followed him to the door. But he kept walking.

"Zach," the admiral called him back once again.

Frustrated by the power play, Zach stopped, but didn't turn around.

"Anytime, day or night and in less than four hours, I can mobilize an entire SEAL team. As soon as this situation has been evaluated, I'll be on it."

Zach did turn around then. "Let me be on that team," he begged. He'd get down on his knees if he had to. His godfather had to see how important this was to him.

"Mitch?" Augusta Dann touched her husband's uniform sleeve. The admiral turned his attention to his wife. "It isn't her," he said in a gentle voice.

"Thank God." Augusta began to sob. "Oh, that poor girl. Her parents…" Her hand went to her throat. "What about our daughter, Mitch? Is she alive?"

"We don't know, Gus."

"But your mobilizing a team? And, Zach—" she turned to look at him "—was leaving in a hurry." She addressed him directly, "You think she's alive. You're going after her."

It wasn't a question, but a statement.

"Zach is not going after *anyone*." Admiral Dann narrowed his gaze on Zach. "He's coming with me. *And that's an order.*"

CHAPTER FIVE

0800 Saturday
Washington, D.C.

THE ADMIRAL'S LIMO driver navigated the streets of the nation's capital until they reached the beltway, then headed south out of the city. Zach continued to stare out the tinted window as Washington monuments gave way to lush green Virginia countryside.

Sitting across from him, his godfather rode in equally brooding silence. But Zach still wasn't ready to forgive him for pulling rank. If the only way out of this situation was to resign his commission and become a civilian, he'd do it in a heartbeat.

And if he wasn't trapped inside this damn moving monstrosity he'd do it right now. In fact, he *would* do it right now.

Zach automatically checked for the scratch pad he wore strapped to his knee while in the cockpit. In his jet he'd always been prepared for any emergency. That didn't seem to be the case these days. "Do you have paper in this car?"

The admiral ripped a piece from the notepad in his Daytimer and handed it to Zach. Then he said, "I don't know why I didn't see it coming. You're adults. You spend time together. You share common interests. I shouldn't be surprised there was something more to it, but I am." The admiral shook his head. "It makes me feel oceans apart from my little girl. And I mean farther than the Arabian Sea. She never once mentioned the two of you were anything more than friends."

The man had thrown him a curveball, and Zach forgot all about writing his resignation. Instead, he took the next at bat. After all, that was what they were really doing in this car, waiting out the silence until one of them opened the lines of communication.

"We were just friends."

At least that's all they'd been for a very long time. Even if he'd wanted more.

And if she cared about him at all, wouldn't that have come across in conversations with her parents? The admiral wasn't the only one who felt that ever-widening gap.

A moot point. Their relationship, past or present, took a back seat to finding her alive and bringing her home.

"I have eyes, Zach. Don't try and pull the wool over them. You've been intimate with my daughter. And as a father, I'm not sure I like that."

"It was a long time ago. We were just kids."

"That I *don't* need to hear," the admiral growled. "This conversation is as awkward for me as it is for you. The thing is, Michelle and I used to be very close. We'd drifted apart over the past year. And if anything's happened to her, I'd at least like to think I knew my own daughter."

The admiral paused to collect his thoughts. "She was struggling with a difficult career decision. Being the father I am, I offered my advice until she was sick of hearing it. I even suggested it was time she settled down. Of course, it came across as just another lecture from the old man and we'd wind up arguing." He looked at Zach. "Ever talk marriage? Kids? Make plans for the future?"

"Not really."

The admiral nodded. "Do you love her, Zach?"

An honest question deserved an honest answer. At least Zach could look him in the eye when he said it. "Yes, sir. I do."

"Does she love you?"

That one was harder to answer. "I don't know."

"Well, why don't you know?"

I don't know.

They lapsed back into silence, more comfortable

than the honesty. Neither had accepted that Michelle might not have a future. Zach's gaze shifted to the window, but he didn't focus, and the trees and foliage passed by in a blur of green.

"Your BUD/S training starts Monday," the admiral said several minutes later.

Safer topic.

"I appreciate the opportunity."

"Like hell you do." The admiral softened the recrimination with a sad smile. "You're just going through the motions. You gotta want it, Zach, for it to mean anything at all. Otherwise it's too easy to give up. That girl loved to fly. You both did. I was surprised you gave up on jets as easily as you did."

"You're disappointed I quit."

"You didn't quit, Zach. You gave up. I can respect a quitter."

So the admiral didn't respect him. "Captain Greene's a good man, Zach. He knew you were in shock when he hauled your ass out of the gulf. Hell, he didn't even press charges after you'd knocked his teeth loose. Just let you cool off your hot head in the brig. But you defied him every step of the way. If you'd have done your time in rehab, we wouldn't be having this conversation right now. I wonder if you have what it takes to make it through SEAL training."

The admiral was right on. What could Zach say? *I don't plan on being around come Monday?*

The admiral checked his watch. "Right about now Team One is debriefing on this latest recon mission. Navy Intel will analyze and strategize, and my boys will be back out there to follow up on any new leads. I'm considering postponing your BUD/S training in favor of a little on-job training by letting you ride along with Team One to the Middle East."

Zach sat up straighter.

"*Considering* it," Admiral Dann cautioned. "I know you want to find Michelle as much as I do. Cool your heels. Stick around town. Wait for cooler heads to prevail. In other words, follow the rules for once. And I might give you that chance. In return I want your total commitment to SEAL training when you get back." He handed Zach a beeper. "Keep this with you 24/7."

"You won't regret it."

"I'd better not."

The limo merged right and slowed as the driver took the off-ramp.

"Where are we headed?" Zach asked. He hadn't given that much thought to their destination.

"To the Daniels family to break the news of their daughter's death."

That caught Zach off guard. "I thought the

chaplain was handling that.'' The admiral had made arrangements with the chaplain's office while at the hospital.

''The chaplain's meeting us there. You were her squad leader, Zach. It's an unpleasant but necessary duty to show them this respect. They'll have questions. Want answers. Want to know about shipboard life. Flying.'' He met Zach's gaze. ''Details concerning your engagement with the MiGs are still classified. So steer clear. That shouldn't be too hard to do if you keep it personal.''

But the admiral hadn't warned him how hard *personal* would get. They'd pulled into the drive at the Danielses' home the same time the chaplain did. Mrs. Daniels met them at the door before they were even out of the cars. By the time they hit the front-porch steps, tears were forming in her eyes. They stepped onto the porch and she began to sob. The sobbing continued out of control.

They hadn't yet said a word.

At the first sight of official-looking cars and three uniformed naval officers, Mrs. Daniels knew that her daughter, Sara, was dead.

It was Mr. Daniels who ushered them inside. Giving his wife time to collect herself, he served iced tea. Mrs. Daniels joined them again a few minutes later. Their son, a high-school senior, arrived home from his Saturday job at a garage.

A nice middle-class American home with a nice middle-class American family. And their daughter didn't deserve to die.

Zach spent the rest of the morning singing Skeeter's praises. And wishing he'd gotten to know her just a little bit better, so he didn't have to fake so many of the answers. He gave the watered down version of their engagement with the enemy fighters, using all the appropriate language to help Sara's grieving family.

"Your daughter died honorably in the line of duty. Her courage and sacrifice are recognized by a grateful nation."

They wanted to know the little things, like what she ate for breakfast. And did the ship really run out of milk? Did she eat her cereal dry? Or with powdered milk? Because she'd never liked powdered milk. Never drank it at home.

He remembered Skeeter pushing away her cereal *that day*. Because of him. Letting them think she'd had a healthy breakfast seemed the humane thing to do. So he didn't tell them she hadn't eaten. Or that she'd never liked him. Or that he could barely stand to be in the same room with her—for no apparent reason other than the subject of Michelle always seemed to come between them.

Had she dated anyone that he knew of? A pilot perhaps? She'd never mentioned a boyfriend.

"Thank you for coming, Chaplain, Admiral...Lieutenant Prince." Mr. Daniels shook their hands in turn, then walked them to the door.

At the door Mrs. Daniels held on to both of Zach's hands as if she didn't want to let him go. "Thank you again for coming, Lieutenant. Sara always spoke so highly of you. She really admired the way you handled a jet."

All morning he'd been fighting to keep down the lump in this throat. It just tripled in size.

"And, Admiral," Mrs. Daniels continued, "I hope the news of your own daughter..." She couldn't bring herself to finish the sentence. "Well, Sara just absolutely *loved* that girl. We'll be praying for Michelle."

1000 Monday
ARLINGTON NATIONAL CEMETERY,
Arlington, VA

FORTY-EIGHT HOURS LATER, Zach was graveside, paying his last respects to Lieutenant Junior Grade Sara Marie Daniels.

Shots rang out in tribute to the fallen navigator.

Uniformed and civilian mourners were gathered around the freshly dug grave site, crowding under black umbrellas. The bleak drizzle matched the mood. Zach let the rain wash over him.

Wash away his sins.

The honor guard folded the flag into a neat triangle and presented it with a salute to the silently weeping Mrs. Daniels, husband and son by her side.

As the Navy chaplain intoned the final benediction, "Ashes to ashes, dust to dust..." Zach's attention shifted to Admiral and Mrs. Dann. Every emotion crossing the Danielses' faces was mirrored in their faces.

And Zach knew exactly how they felt.

He didn't want to be standing here again.

Zach heard the jet engines just before the planes broke through the clouds. Four F/A-18 Hornets from their ship's Air Wing zoomed by overhead. The lag jet banked and dropped out of formation. *Missing Man.*

A tribute to Sara.

But the real missing "man" was Michelle.

The visual hit Zach right in the solar plexus.

"You want to go get a beer at the Officers' Club?" Steve Marietta, his old RIO, came up and put his arm around Zach's shoulder. "I told the guys we'd meet 'em there." Steve nodded toward the sky, indicating the pilots of the Hornets. His old running mates.

God, that seemed like a lifetime ago.

"A little early to be drinking," Zach hedged. He really wanted this drink. "Sure, why the hell not."

They drove to Andrews Air Force Base in Steve's rental car. Zach hadn't bothered with transportation. He didn't plan on hanging around long enough. They parked outside the Officers' Club and went inside. This early in the day the lights were up. Some country-and-western singer crooned her latest hit from the jukebox in the corner. Cue balls and beer bottles clinked out their own brand of music.

There were a few casual drinkers in the place.

Mostly Air Force, but a few other branches. No "loose" women. Not even a female officer. Not like the bars back home.

There was the usual good-natured ribbing when they walked in with their Navy uniforms on.

"You know why Navy pilots have to take off and land on boats?" some smart-ass shouted from across the room. Then answered it himself. "Because they can't fly fast enough or far enough."

"Yeah, well, that's not what your sister said when I was stoking her burners," Steve shot back.

"Steve, he's going to come over here and kick your ass. And I'm going to let him," Zach warned.

But the guy didn't do anything.

"Just a bunch of wussies. My kind of place,"
Steve said loud enough for their audience to hear.
He cracked his knuckles.

Zach shook his head. "Why don't you just mark
your territory, Steve?"

"I think I will. Order up two beers, will ya? I
gotta check out the head."

Zach sat down at the bar. "Two beers. A round
of your best scotch for the room. And a full bottle
right here."

"Who died?" the bartender asked, wiping down
the bar and setting out two napkins for coasters.

"Skeeter Daniels. My wingman's RIO. Shot
down over Iraq."

With the rag in his hand the bartender pointed
at Zach. "You're that Navy hotshot, aren't you. I
heard you took on three MiGs in a Tomcat. Then
landed your crippled jet on the deck of an aircraft
carrier with nothing but fumes in the tank." The
bartender reached into a refrigerator under the bar
and set down two bottles of beer.

"Flew jets myself in Vietnam. On the house,
Ace."

Zach looked down at the beer in his hand. He'd
had seven kills. Two more than he needed for Ace.
Few pilots reached that distinction in their careers.
But the guy had the story all wrong. "That's just

the fairy-tale version. I ditched the plane in the ocean. It ran out of gas. They don't give you any medals for that.''

''Yeah, but the part about the three MiGs is right, isn't it?''

Zach nodded.

''Coming right up on the rest of those drinks.'' The bartender left him alone with his thoughts and his beer. Zach pushed the bottle aside without taking a drink.

He and Steve had been pulled out of the water several hours later—after the search and rescue for Rapunzel and Skeeter was well under way. The first SEAL recon team dispatched to the crash site reported that the Tomcat had disintegrated on impact.

No recoverable munitions.

No bodies. No tracking signals.

And no faction, hostile or otherwise, ever came forward claiming hostages.

Missing in action, presumed dead.

He'd no longer presume anything.

Steve returned. Took a swig of his beer. ''Thanks.'' He saluted with the bottle. ''And thanks to you and those three MiGs you shot down…that day, I'm getting my shot as a retread. Got orders to train with the F/A-18 Hornets.''

"I'm happy for you, Steve."

"But you're not happy, are you, Ace. Feel kind of guilty myself, you know?"

Zach didn't have to answer. They both knew what he meant. When had they started referring to it as *that day?* As if everything that should follow those two words had never happened. *That day your wingman was shot down.*

By the time the bartender finished passing out the round of scotch, their Air Wing arrived, making the bar fifty-fifty Air Force and Navy.

The bartender handed the open bottle of scotch to Zach. "On the house."

"Thanks." Zach poured it out onto the polished bar surface, creating a stream that ran the length of the bar. Then he lifted his shot glass. "To Sara Daniels!"

"To Sara," Air Force and Navy echoed in salute to their fallen comrade.

Zach lit the liquor trail at one end. The alcohol ignited. Flames danced along the surface to the other. They tipped their shots.

This drink was for Sara.

The liquid fire burned in his belly. And burned along the bar until all that was left of their tribute was another char line.

Zach's pager beeped.

1300 Monday
PENTAGON NAVY ANNEX,
Washington, D.C.

"GENTLEMEN, let's not stand on formality. We all know why we're here." Admiral Dann stood at the head of the conference table in a large sealed-off room in the basement of the Pentagon-Navy Annex. "Please take your seats."

Settling into one of the plush leather chairs, Zach popped a piece of Bazooka in his mouth and looked around the room. With one phone call and in considerably less than four hours, the admiral had indeed amassed a roomful of Navy SEALs and intelligence officers. Though Zach had the impression this wasn't the first time a special task force had convened in the past month.

There were commanders from SEAL teams Seven, Six, Four, Two and One. They had names like Cage, DJ, Animal and the Exterminator. Brad Bailey, commanding officer of Team One, and Marc, had flown in from California without so much as a hint of their business with the admiral. As the CO of SEAL training, one of the most important aspects of his brother-in-law's job was causality assessment.

While Zach had spent a month wasting time as a disorderly drunk, the admiral had been busy. But every minute spent in this room was another minute wasted. Sand poured from the hourglass. Zach didn't know how much time he had. Only that he intended to make the most of it.

"Sorry I'm late." A soft-spoken commander, looking very much out of place among the kick-ass Navy SEAL brass, entered the room. The marine posted outside the door had allowed him access.

"Come in, Chaplain," Admiral Dann said. "We were just getting started. Gentlemen, I'd like you to meet Chaplain Rashad Abd al Matin. Commander Matin is our resident expert in Muslim studies and the Middle East."

Chaplain Matin sank into the nearest empty seat as the admiral continued around the room with introductions. "I think everyone here knows the retired Captain Prince either by association or reputation. I've invited him to sit in as a special adviser to these proceedings. *Lieutenant* Prince, our newest BUD/S recruit, is here strictly as an observer." Admiral Dann pinned Zach with his stare, letting him know he should feel privileged to even be there.

He and the admiral had come to an understanding of sorts. He'd agreed to stay for the briefing. And the admiral agreed not to courtmartial his insubordinate ass.

In other words, he didn't have a choice.

If he played by the rules for a change, as soon

as the meeting adjourned, he'd be on the next flight to the Middle East with the rest of them.

The admiral's aide, Alan Ogden, moved around the table, passing out folders marked TOP SE-CRET. Maybe the briefing wouldn't be a waste of his time, after all.

"I see the party's started without me." A brash young "suit" slipped into the room just as the marine moved to secure the double wide doors. A female lieutenant commander followed hot on his heels.

"Chester 'Chess' McKenna, Central Intelligence Agency. And Dr. Sloan Trahern, Psych Ops." The admiral acknowledged the latecomers, and the marine allowed the pair to pass unchallenged. "I didn't know you were back from the Middle East, McKenna."

"Came straight from the airport. You want me at this party, Mitch," McKenna said with deliberate disregard for military protocol. He tossed a four-inch-thick folder onto the table and handed a videotape to the admiral's aide.

"I've asked Dr. Trahern to consult because of the nature of this tape."

"Token female," the doctor said, depositing a slide projector and other visual aids onto the table. She sat down in the seat across from Zach.

McKenna remained standing. "I heard your guys recovered a body?"

"The RIO, Sara Daniels," the admiral confirmed.

Ogden aide handed McKenna the remote control to the television set. "Have a seat, Mitch," McKenna said. "You're going to want to see this tape sitting down."

McKenna clicked the play button.

Michelle's battered and bruised face appeared on the TV screen. The room became deathly quiet. The expensive upholstery creaked beneath Zach's uneasy movements as he leaned forward in his seat.

"You can see by the dated tape that this was made five days after your daughter's plane crashed ten miles outside of Arbil, Iraq, approximately one hundred miles from the Turkish boarder." McKenna adjusted the volume.

"Lieutenant Michelle Dann, United States Navy," she said to the camera. Michelle wore her flight suit and looked straight into the lens with a discipline that burned through brown eyes Zach remembered so well. But she had difficulty speaking because of a swollen cheek and split lip.

What had they done to her?

Her gaze shifted to the paper in her hand. "I renounce my country, the capitalist United States

of America, her capitalist president, her government and her people for crimes committed against
a peaceful Islam. Free my Shiite brother, Sadiq al
Mukhtar, from your prisons or suffer the consequences as foretold by the prophet Mohammed.''

The tape rolled over to static.

Zach could barely contain himself. He wanted
to crawl over the table, reach into that TV monitor
and bring her home where she belonged.

Everyone in the room remained silent a few seconds longer. It was obvious the statement had been
beaten out of her. Not a man among this roomful
of battle-scared combat veterans wanted to see a
woman treated that way.

Then everyone sitting around the table began
talking at once. *Where is she? Who's holding her?*
The same questions raced through Zach's mind
along with about a dozen others.

How soon can I leave to go get her?

''Are we holding a terrorist by the name Sadiq
al Mukhtar?'' Team Seven's commander asked.

''We're holding him, but not as a terrorist,'' Mc-
Kenna answered. ''Sadiq al Mukhtar was picked
up for drug trafficking in New York a few months
ago. Convicted and sentenced to fifteen years.''
McKenna passed around an eight-by-ten blowup of
a mug shot. ''He should never have been allowed
in the U.S. We can place this guy in the city of

every major international terrorist incident spanning the last two decades.'' McKenna knuckled the folder in front of him. "Sadiq has long been a suspect in the bombing of the Marine Corps barracks in Beirut. This guy is one bad dude.''

"Obviously we're not going to release him,'' the CO of SEAL Team Two added.

"We can't. A week ago Sadiq sent word to our agency that he wanted to deal. He was knifed to death in a prison fight before we ever got a chance to talk to him. Someone didn't want us to hear what this guy had to say.''

"So some person or group connected to Mukhtar is holding Michelle?'' Zach asked. He looked from McKenna to the admiral. His godfather stared at the open file in front of him, listening but removed from the conversation going on around the room.

"Or they've killed her,'' Team leader Four said. "If this guy is dead, they don't need her anymore.''

Zach glared at the man responsible for the comment, a captain sitting to the right of Dr. Trahern.

The doctor looked equally uncomfortable with the soldier's assessment. "She's more valuable alive than dead.''

"We have reason to believe she's still alive.'' McKenna stated.

Zach's heart pounded. He knew it to be true. And not just because he wanted it to be true.

Michelle was a survivor.

"Did everyone catch the 'free my brother,' on the tape?" McKenna continued. "Sadiq considered himself the chosen one. But he was an extremist with few followers left even among his own tribe, though he did have at least one brother living in Iraq. We think this brother was responsible for making the tape. We have a satellite photo of Ihassan Mukhtar near Karbala, Iraq, yesterday morning." McKenna flipped on the slide projector and impatiently waved the admiral's aide toward the light. Then the agent clicked through several slides of an Arab in black robes standing near a white van, each one increasing in size until the picture focused on the man's thin face.

A face that looked enough like the one in the mug shot for them to believe they were indeed brothers.

"My team's ready to go. Let's move on Karbala and bag these guys," Brad Bailey said.

"I'm afraid someone beat you to it." McKenna brought up a slide of two dead bodies. "Ali Ra'id. We've identified the other man as being from the al Ra'id tribe. Ra'id and al Mukhtar served and deserted the Iraqi Republican Guard. It's possible Ra'id adopted the al Mukhtar tribe as his own. In connection with the death of Sadiq, I dispatched one of our shadow operatives to the area as soon as I confirmed the satellite photo. Both Arabs were dead when the agent arrived. Bodies still warm.

"My man found this tape, made but never circulated. Perhaps awaiting word from Sadiq. There was evidence someone had been held hostage in the basement where the men were found. We think that someone was Michelle Dann." He dumped the contents of a small manila envelope on the table. A single dog tag fell out, along with Michelle's leather wings.

Zach automatically reached out for the strip of leather that had been ripped from her uniform. He remembered her touch down after that first solo flight. He'd soloed earlier that same day and had waited around for her to finish. She'd walked off the flight line straight toward him with a big smile on her face.

And when she took off her helmet and whipped that full head of hair around like someone in a shampoo commercial, he knew right then she'd passed.

"Nice going, Rapunzel," he'd said, tagging her with the call sign.

Then their instructor had come along and ruined the moment. "Yeah, nice solo, Rapunzel." He'd patted her bottom in passing.

"Hey, asshole!" Zach had challenged him.

The guy turned. "I know you're not talking to me, hotshot."

"Zach, please." Michelle held him back.

"Are you just gonna put up with that?"

She turned on him. "Are you just now noticing what I have to put up with?"

"If you don't report that guy, I will."

"You'll only make it worse. I can handle it!"

That was in the days before the Tailhook scandal, before sexual harassment became politically incorrect. And that was when Zach realized she was so desperate for acceptance from these guys, she'd put up with anything.

His fist closed over the worn leather.

She'd earned her wings, the hard way.

But somewhere along the line Michelle *had* learned to handle it by being cool under fire, whether the barrage came from a 20-mm canon or the mouth of some insensitive jerk.

She'd never gained their acceptance. But she'd earned their respect.

Zach was counting on the fact that Michelle knew how to hang tough.

Just a little while longer, sweetheart.

He clenched his jaw around the question he was afraid to ask but wanted to know the answer to just the same.

The admiral spoke for them all. "Who has her now?"

"We're not one hundred percent sure. Just how resourceful is that daughter of yours, Mitch?"

"Very!" the admiral answered.

Brad Bailey spoke up. "Enough to bury her RIO so that the grave wouldn't be stumbled upon by some shepherd out for a Sunday stroll. We missed it the first several passes, which is why we never recovered the body before now."

McKenna nodded. "Here's where it gets really interesting." He freed a photo from another manila envelope. "This morning's satellite pass of Saudi Arabia, several hundred miles southwest of Iraq. A real hot spot we've been keeping an eye on. I didn't have time to get the picture made into a slide," he apologized, handing it to the admiral.

The admiral pushed to his feet. "Why the hell didn't you show me this first?"

"I thought it was more dramatic my way. We don't have the whole story. But we do have a problem here, Mitch. Yesterday your daughter was missing in action. Today she's right in the middle of it. And we have no idea how long she's actually been free. As of 0855 this morning, Lieutenant Michelle Dann is on the CIA's most wanted list of terrorists."

The admiral threw the photo onto the middle of

the table. Zach and the rest of the room got a good look at Michelle in black robes, toting a Russian-made AK-47, running headlong through a Bedouin camp. He could sense her movement, feel her urgency in the still photo.

"Are you implying my daughter is a rogue warrior?"

"She's wearing the robes of the al Mukhtar. The tribes have very distinctive dress, which is how they identify friend from foe. She's in the camp of their enemy carrying an assault weapon during a raid. We just want to find out why."

No shit. The understatement of the year! Zach hung on the man's every word. But didn't believe for a minute the man's assumption that Michelle was a terrorist.

"She's wearing a dead man's robes," his dad spoke up. "Click back to the picture of the guy by the van."

McKenna complied.

"Now ahead to the slide of the dead guy. What happened to his clothes? Take a good look at what your fugitive is wearing. You'll notice a dark stain about chest high. She's not bleeding from a chest wound." Tad Prince's mouth curled into a smile. McKenna had missed that small detail, and his dad was only too happy to point it out.

"You want me to believe that in the last forty-eight hours Michelle Dann broke out of her prison, scrounged an assault weapon, took out two bad guys and escaped Iraq into the desert of Saudi Arabia? Where, I might add, she just happened to stumble into the camp of the al Ra'id wearing the robes of their enemy—and they didn't kill her?''

"You have a better explanation?'' Admiral Dann asked. "Because I'd really like to hear it.''

Dr. Trahern spoke up. "Although I don't agree with Chester, I think what he's trying to say, Admiral, is that he believes your daughter never escaped the al Mukhtar, but rather joined them.

"Shades of Patty Hearst. It's not unusual for captives to bond with their captors. Under extreme conditions it becomes a means to endure the abuse.''

"There are more al Mukhtar tribesmen out there. Not to mention the al Ra'id,'' McKenna added. "We don't know that these two were the only ones in contact with her. And because she's a woman—''

"Not *because* she's a woman,'' Dr. Trahern interjected. "The phenomenon is known as the Stockholm syndrome. In 1973 four Swedes held in a bank vault for six days during an unsuccessful robbery attempt became very attached to the robbers. I'm sure you're familiar with the case and others like it, Admiral.''

"Yes, thank you, Sloan, for reminding us. Everyone here has heard of the Stockholm syndrome." The admiral and his father exchanged looks. "Let's just say I buy into your theory, McKenna—"

"There's no other explanation," McKenna interrupted.

"I don't give a damn what the explanation is. I'm sending a team in after my daughter. Alan—" the admiral addressed his aide "—I want this morning's crop of satellite photos. Anything within a hundred-mile radius of this one."

"Already on it, sir."

"Marc, brainstorm a contingency plan and a backup. I want it within the hour. Brad, your entire team is on standby. Have them ready to move within four."

Marc nodded.

Brad responded enthusiastically. "You've got it."

"Admiral?" Zach pushed to his feet.

He didn't need to ask. The admiral already knew what he wanted.

"All right, Zach. You can ride along with Team One, but you're to stick to the background."

"I'm afraid I can't let you mobilize to the area," McKenna said. "The al Ra'id and the al Mukhtar are at war. The U.S. has to appear neutral." Mc-

Kenna stood his ground in the face of several angry Navy SEALs ready to defend their admiral's honor, Zach being one of them. How dare the agent contradict the admiral's orders just when Zach had gotten his godfather to concede.

"I don't recall asking your permission, Agent McKenna."

"That's why I went over your head, Mitch, to the Chief of Special Operations Command. The CIA is charged with this mission, not the Navy SEALs. There's someone missing from this puzzle, someone higher up the food chain than Sadiq Mukhtar, someone who wanted him dead.

"I believe your daughter has led us straight to him. We don't care about the three dead terrorists. We want al Ra'id!" McKenna spoke passionately.

"Would you mind if I interjected something here, gentlemen?" the soft-spoken chaplain asked. "Khanh Asad al Ra'id is not a terrorist. Prince Asad can trace his bloodline back to Moorish kings. He's considered a leader of his people. They call him the Lion Prince of the Desert."

"We're aware of that, Chaplain," McKenna said. "We're not trying to pin two decades of terrorism on this guy. But if his reach extends from the Middle East to North America, we want to know about it."

McKenna rubbed a hand across the back of his

neck as if he was growing increasingly hot under the collar of that starched white shirt. "We can't risk offending the al Ra'id with a rescue operation."

"You'd sacrifice my daughter for some damn CIA recruiting mission?" The admiral advanced on him.

McKenna took a step backward. "Even I'm not that heartless."

"Alan, get me the Chief of SpecOps on the horn," the admiral ordered.

"That won't be necessary, Mitch. I'm willing to concede the point and send a Navy SEAL in after her. Just one unarmed man. Keep it low-key and friendly."

"What's the catch? Besides being unarmed. If the CIA is in charge of this operation, why aren't you sending in one of your own?"

"I've never had an operative return from that particular part of the Arabian desert. It's known as the Rub'al-Khali, Empty Quarter, the largest stretch of desert in Saudi Arabia."

The admiral cursed under his breath.

"Your guy paves the way for my guy."

"Unarmed," Marc interjected. "That's suicide."

In the end every SEAL in the room volunteered, including his outspoken brother-in-law. Zach didn't have a chance of being assigned the job among all the experienced volunteers in the room.

He only knew he had to be.

He made eye contact with McKenna. No one in the room liked the man. But Zach was about to become his new best friend.

"I'm going myself," Admiral Dann announced, putting an end to the discussion and a crimp in Zach's plans.

"Actually you were our second choice, Admiral," Dr. Trahern dared to tell him. "We even considered the retired Captain Prince because of his psychology degree. To put it bluntly, sir, under these conditions, if your daughter is under the influence of these men, you want someone who knows her better than she knows herself."

"What in the hell kind of psychobabble is that?"

Zach looked into McKenna's eyes and knew...

"We've chosen Lieutenant Prince for the job," McKenna said.

"You can't send Zach. He hasn't even been through the first training phase."

"I have the authority to dip into SEALs." McKenna asserted. "As of 0700 this morning, he's one of your boys."

"Why not send in a SEAL specially trained in hostage negotiation and deprogramming?"

"He wouldn't have the advantage of knowing your daughter the way I do. If you'll forgive me for saying so, sir." Zach shifted his attention to his godfather. He'd beg if he had to. "I'm the man for this mission. You might even say I was born for it."

CHAPTER SIX

AL RA'ID BEDOUIN CAMP,
Saudi Arabia

"MAY I COME IN?" Asad asked, lifting the tent flap and entering at her nod. "How are you feeling today?"

"Still fuzzy," she responded, sitting up in her bed of sheepskins. And a little guilty for having taken over his bed. His tent. And his life so completely. Khanh Asad and his people had been more than kind to her since her arrival in their Bedouin camp. Especially since she was still covered in filth. And smelled worse than his whole herd of camels combined. "How long have I been out?"

"Two days."

"What?" She'd arrived bone-weary, but he hadn't allowed her to sleep those first twelve hours because of the bump on her forehead. She touched it gingerly and winced. Asad had cleaned and dressed the gash with butterfly tape. "Forty-eight hours?"

"What does it matter?" he said kindly. "You needed your rest." He moved to her bedside with a cup of coffee. "*El-heif,* first cup. Drink." In the Bedouin tradition her host took a sip first, then offered the cup to her. Their way of letting strangers know it was safe. And she did feel safe here. Perhaps the safest she'd felt in a very long time.

If only she could remember who she was running from. And why. Then maybe she could remember her own name.

"Thank you." She took the cup of coffee, amazed that after one taste she knew she liked hers strong and black. The aroma triggered another fainter memory of a coffee shop.

In her own neighborhood? One she visited occasionally or frequently? Or the image of one on every street corner, an association from an advertising blitz?

She didn't know.

"Would you care to break your fast?"

"I'm not really very hungry."

"You will soon regain your appetite and your memory. In the meantime, perhaps we can piece this puzzle together." Asad sat down next to her and picked up the discarded robes she'd been wearing when she'd stumbled into the al Ra'id camp two days ago. "Aside from the fact that the robes belong to the al Mukhtar and you are definitely not of their blood, I think we can assume they are not yours.'' He stuck his finger through the bullet hole of the bloodstained robes for emphasis, then tossed the garments aside.

At least she hadn't been shot, but she had been wearing a vest, holstering a 9-mm handgun. And toting an AK-47 assault weapon.

Did that make her the shooter?

She toyed with the zipper of the jumper she'd fallen asleep in. Some kind of uniform or work clothes, worn underneath the robes. Also bloodstained and much too big for her. A man's jumper. ''I don't think these are mine, either.''

Asad looked at her thoughtfully for a moment. ''Perhaps not.'' But he didn't sound as sure as she did. And she wasn't sure about anything at all. ''I found these things in the pocket of the black robes.'' He spread an array of items across her lap.

She picked up a ring first thing. A small diamond set in a plain gold band. She studied it thoughtfully with no recollection of how it had come to be in her possession. She looked down at her left hand, tried to imagine it there—and couldn't.

''I do not think you are a married woman. Or even betrothed. No tan line,'' he said, pointing out the obvious.

But when she tried it on her finger, the diamond

fit. If the ring was hers, why hadn't she been wearing it? If it wasn't...

"A thief perhaps?" Asad teased.

Had she stolen it? Why would she do such a thing? Was she someone of low moral character? Perhaps something worse than a thief. A murderer? A thief and a murderer? Is that why she was wearing bloodstained, bullet-riddled clothes and running for her life?

No, no...she couldn't even comprehend committing such acts.

"I don't honestly know." But she preferred to believe she was engaged. She placed the ring on her finger and picked up the next item. A printed card. With both English and Arabic writing. She'd discovered earlier that she could understand the Arabic language, even speak a little, but she couldn't read it. "What is it?"

"Some sort of communication aid. The Arabic translates the English phrase. As is this," he said, picking up a cloth printed with an American flag. "It promises great rewards for helping the bearer to safety."

She stared at the items without comprehension. "Am I that bearer?"

He nodded in that thought-provoking way of his. "I think we can also assume you are an American." He picked up a red, white and blue patch and matched it to the threaded outline on the shoulder of the jumper.

Stars and Stripes. Old Glory.

The Star Spangled Banner.

Yes, she knew without doubt she was a United States citizen. Where was her passport? Her identification?

Driver's license? Military ID?

"So what are you doing in the Arabian desert?" Asad echoed her thoughts.

"I don't know," she answered earnestly.

"A while back there were rumors of an attack by two U.S. fighters shot down over Iraq. The pilots were reported killed. And the Iraqi celebrated a great victory. The U.S. claimed the incident started over Kuwaiti airspace. Both sides settled the matter without further incident."

"Who's your rumor control?"

"CNN."

"Still, I'm not a fighter pilot," she said, laughing off the suggestion. "I know the inside of a cockpit like I know my own name, *not*." She brought the coffee cup to her lips and took another sip.

"Hmm…perhaps not. But you are dressed like one. And how would you explain these?" He held up a set of dog tags.

She reached for them and read the names. "Sara

Daniels. Michelle Dann.'' Didn't they come in pairs? Wouldn't they be the same?

"My understanding is you take one and leave the other with the body," Asad explained.

"But there's only one of each."

"So which dead woman are you?"

An image flashed. She could feel the chain tightening around her throat until she couldn't breathe. In the next instant she was the one yanking the chain free from around someone else's neck.

She shook her head to clear it.

Asad searched her brown eyes with his darker ones.

"What did you remember?"

"Nothing," she whispered. What didn't she *want* to remember? was a better question.

He let the chain slip from his hand into her lap, along with the rest of her life's story. If only she could make sense of it all.

"All the pieces are there. You have to want to put them together." His nomadic wisdom seemed far beyond that of his thirty-some years, perhaps passed down from generation upon generation of tribesmen. He had the dark exotic looks of his Moorish ancestors. And she could easily picture him at home in his desert surroundings. But his clothes were modern and his manners that of a well-bred gentleman.

An intriguing combination.

She broke eye contact and stared, unseeing, into the coffee cup in her hands. "You think I'm one of those American fighter pilots? Then why isn't my country searching for me?"

"Perhaps it is."

She picked up the dog tags again, turned them over in her hand. "Sara." She had a very strong gut-level association with the name. "I think…I'm Sara." She shook her head. "No, it doesn't sound right. But I remember Sara, not a face, but a feeling."

"What about Michelle?"

"No, nothing."

"There is an American embassy in Riyadh. I can get in touch with your people though e-mail…"

A very real and unexplained fear closed off her throat at the thought of leaving this safe haven. She reached out and touched his hand. "Asad, I wish you wouldn't." Did that make her a traitor? A deserter?

"A man cannot escape his past. But in the desert a man's past does not always matter. It is the same for a woman. We have much in common, I think." He pushed to his feet. "You may stay under the protection of the al Ra'id as long as you wish, Sara Michelle. Or you are free to go and I will provide the transportation. The choice is yours."

"I'd like to stay. For a while," she added, suspecting she sounded too eager.

He nodded. "As you wish." He bowed his head slightly. "A new life calls for a new name. You shall be reborn in the Muslim tradition. I will call you Kalilah. Kalilah al Ra'id."

"Kalilah al Ra'id." She tested the sound of her new name. "What does it mean?"

He hesitated. "Darling or sweetheart of the leader."

Her pulse skipped a beat. Darling, sweetheart. She liked the sound of it. Maybe a little bit too much, considering he was the leader of this particular camp.

She twisted the ring on her finger.

"And darling," he teased, "I don't know how to break this to you. But you need a bath. To put it in plain English. You stink."

WITH THE BASIN of water Asad had provided, she attempted to make herself presentable. But only made matters worse. She'd have to get used to wearing her debris-matted hair in dreadlocks. It became mud-caked around her freshly washed face. And hopelessly beyond combing.

She angled Asad's shaving mirror to get a better look at herself. A stranger stared back. Not a single

The Harlequin Reader Service® — Here's how it works:

Accepting your 2 free books and gift places you under no obligation to buy anything. You may keep the books and gift and return the shipping statement marked "cancel." If you do not cancel, about a month later we'll send you 6 additional novels and bill you just $3.80 each in the U.S., or $4.21 each in Canada, plus 25¢ shipping & handling per book and applicable taxes if any.* That's the complete price and — compared to cover prices of $4.50 each in the U.S. and $5.25 each in Canada — it's quite a bargain! You may cancel at any time, but if you choose to continue, every month we'll send you 6 more books, which you may either purchase at the discount price or return to us and cancel your subscription.

*Terms and prices subject to change without notice. Sales tax applicable in N.Y. Canadian residents will be charged applicable provincial taxes and GST.

NO POSTAGE
NECESSARY
IF MAILED
IN THE
UNITED STATES

BUSINESS REPLY MAIL
FIRST-CLASS MAIL   PERMIT NO. 717   BUFFALO, NY

POSTAGE WILL BE PAID BY ADDRESSEE

HARLEQUIN READER SERVICE
3010 WALDEN AVE
PO BOX 1867
BUFFALO NY 14240-9952

If offer card is missing write to: Harlequin Reader Service., 3010 Walden Ave., P.O. Box 1867, Buffalo NY 14240-1867

Play The **Lucky Hearts** Game

and get...

FREE BOOKS & a FREE GIFT... YOURS to KEEP!

Yes! I have scratched off the silver card. Please send me my **2 FREE BOOKS** and **FREE MYSTERY GIFT**. I understand that I am under no obligation to purchase any books as explained on the back of this card.

Scratch Here! then look below to see what your cards get you...

336 HDL DC3X   **135 HDL DC3N**

NAME   (PLEASE PRINT CLEARLY)

ADDRESS

APT.#   CITY

STATE/PROV.   ZIP/POSTAL CODE

 Twenty-one gets you **2 FREE BOOKS** and a **FREE MYSTERY GIFT!**

 Twenty gets you **2 FREE BOOKS!**

 Nineteen gets you **1 FREE BOOK!**

 TRY AGAIN!

Offer limited to one per household and not valid to current Harlequin Superromance® subscribers. All orders subject to approval.

 Visit us online at **www.eHarlequin.com**

DETACH AND MAIL CARD TODAY! (H-SR-0S-04/01)

© 1998 HARLEQUIN ENTERPRISES LTD. ® and ™ are trademarks owned by Harlequin Enterprises Limited.

recognizable feature in her drawn face. Who was she?

A fighter pilot? Sara? Michelle?

Someone's fiancée?

Sun-damaged skin flaked on her nose. But aside from multiplying freckles, her sunburn had already begun to fade. Also fading were bruises and telltale abrasions, reminding her, along with the gash on her forehead, she didn't want to go back to wherever the hell she'd come from. Clearly she'd taken a beating from more than just the elements.

She shivered. Was this person or persons likely to come after her again? Scrubbing her body with what remained of the now-filthy bathwater, her limbs went from being dirt-covered to streaked with mud. And kept getting worse. Until she finally gave up. To top it off she had nothing to wear other than the dirty, bloodstained clothes.

Arduously she put the jumper back on. Hesitating a moment more before adding the vest and handgun. Next she slipped her feet into sandals more than a size too big. As an afterthought she hung the dog tags around her neck.

All in all she sure didn't look like something stepping off the pages of the latest issue of *Cosmopolitan* magazine.

When she dared poke her head out of the tent, Asad had the audacity to laugh at her. As did other members of the tribe, including several children who got a real kick out of tugging on her outfit and scurrying away.

"They have never seen such clothes on a woman," Asad explained.

Indeed, the women around camp wore decorative black garments, real gold jewelry proudly displayed on their necks and wrists. Their heads and faces were protected by a plain black scarf called a *bourque*. One of the elderly women offered her a scarf, which she gladly accepted.

When she added it to her ensemble, more peals of laughter followed. She joined in the merriment and didn't mind that the joke was on her. It just felt good to laugh again. To be near children. She didn't think she'd been this content in a very long time.

However, with the *bourque* in place, she could no longer ignore her itching scalp. "I need delousing," she whined to her host.

"Come, I will take you to the wells. My men are filling the water tankers, but they won't be back this way again for several days."

He led the way along the outskirts of the encampment to one of several dune buggies parked beside a herd of ninety or more camels and maybe thirty or so tethered Arabian horses.

"Buckle up," he said, climbing into the driver's seat.

She ducked under the roll bar on the passenger side. "I didn't know itinerant tribes rode around in dune buggies."

"Wake up, Sleeping Beauty," he teased. "It is, after all, the dawn of a new century."

"Why did you call me that?"

Asad turned to look at her. Sincerity replaced his teasing smile. "I apologize for my poor attempt at humor, Kalilah."

"No, I didn't mean that." She dropped the subject. What *did* she mean? As he started up the buggy, she studied Asad's profile with a very real sense of déjà vu. She'd heard that line, or one just like it before.

Sleeping Beauty, Cinderella—she could list all the most common fairy tales. She also knew she didn't put much stock in them or happily-ever-afters.

She touched her thumb to the ring on her finger. Then why get engaged?

"Khanh!" A young woman in a plain black gown came running toward them.

Asad made a U-turn and pulled up alongside her.

"She'll want these," she said shyly, holding up a cloth-wrapped bundle.

"Thank you, Raja." Asad took the parcel from

the woman and deposited what appeared to be toiletries in her lap. "Raja, Kalilah," he introduced them.

"Yes, thank you, Raja." The women exchanged smiles, and the dune buggy roared away.

Nearing midday and several sand dunes later, the novelty of riding helter-skelter through the desert gave way to the reality of a blistering hot day. The mercury topped one hundred degrees. Asad had explained to her that his Bedouin people often rested during the day, saving activity for the morning and evening hours.

Finally the dunes gave way to hard-packed sand and then what appeared to be a small oasis on the horizon.

"Is it real?" she asked, aware of the tricks heat could play on the eyes. When hot air came in contact with an even hotter surface, it created heat waves. Heat waves created an illusion of a wet surface. Mix in a little imagination or a lot of dehydration, and you had a hallucination. Or rather, a mirage.

"See for yourself," he answered.

As they drew nearer, she could make out two tanker trucks and a Humvee a few hundred yards from the watering hole.

"It's beautiful," she said, unbuckling and standing in the seat of the moving vehicle for a better look. "Why don't you camp near here?"

"Because we would trample its beauty beneath our feet."

They pulled up next to the black Hummer, and Asad exchanged greeting in Arabic with a couple of armed tribesmen. One of the men climbed into the lead truck and pulled away from what appeared to be a well, while the other truck took its place. She watched with fascination as the men worked together to lower a pump in preparation for filling the second tanker from the underground water source.

"A bath or a shower?" Asad asked, grabbing a gym bag and the bundle of borrowed toiletries from the back of the dune buggy.

"You mean I have a choice? By all means a shower," she said, enjoying this new adventure.

Asad waved to the driver of the filled tanker, and a few minutes later she was standing under a tepid spray. They'd jerry-rigged a three-sided canvas drape about neck high at the side of the truck, where a long pipe with a showerhead on the end could be turned on and off by a valve. Asad stood guard over her modesty with his back to her.

Not wanting to waste the water or impose on his generosity, she hurried through her shower. When it came to her hair, however, it was clear there was only one solution. She brushed the long rope over her shoulder, bringing to mind another fairy tale. Rapunzel. A princess locked in a tower.

Her lover climbed up her hair to visit her. Funny how neither of them had thought of cutting it to make a rope that would let her climb to freedom.

"Cut it!" she ordered as if she were the witch in the fairy tale. Did that mean her prince wandered the desert blind in search of her?

Turning off the water so as not to waste it, she waited for Asad to return with scissors he'd assured her he carried in his gym bag along with a change of clothes and a few personal items. Such as the razor she'd borrowed to shave her legs and under her arms.

She stood with her back pressed to the canvas.

He grabbed a hunk of hair. "Are you sure?" She could hear the skepticism in his voice.

"No." She laughed, shaking her head. "Just cut."

"Hold still."

She felt the tug. Heard the snip, then another, and another as the weight fell away. Finally she was able to wash her hair, first with strong lye soap to get rid of any lice, then with the bottles of homemade shampoo and conditioner Raja had provided.

When she turned off the water this time, he handed her a nice thick towel to rub down with.

Afterward, she tucked it around her body and stepped from behind the canvas. It felt wonderfully freeing to be able to run her fingers through her short crop of clean hair.

"How do you like it?" she asked, shaking her damp head from side to side.

He started at her hair, but his gaze drifted downward to her towel-wrapped body. "Kalilah, you are as bold as a man," Asad said. Though he didn't seem to fault her for it.

And she felt quite comfortable acting that way.

"May I borrow some clean clothes from your bag?"

"Stay. I will get what you need."

But he only moved closer. Then neither of them moved at all. Her gaze shifted from his lips to the desire burning in his eyes to his lips again. Would he kiss her? Did she want him to?

She brushed her thumb across the ring. Her single anchor to reality. At the moment she felt naked and vulnerable, rather than bold. She broke eye contact with Asad.

He reached up to brush her shorn hair from the butterfly bandage on her forehead. "I don't think you should have gotten it wet."

"My badge of honor. Germans used to wet their dueling scratches in order to leave scars."

"And how would you know that?"

"You have CNN. And I have the History Channel."

"You Americans and your TV."

"My...my mother's German. A naturalized American." She surprised herself by remembering that detail. "If I close my eyes I can hear the soft burr of her accent." She closed her eyes. "I can't picture her face—just a vague image, really. She's calling my name, but I pretend I can't hear her. I'm a little girl and I'm hiding. I don't want to go home because I know I'm in trouble." She felt the burning behind her closed lids and opened them. Blinking back the tears, she choked back a sob.

"And I have a friend who's always in trouble. He studies World War I German flying aces. A pilot, I think. At least, he likes to think of himself as a renegade Red Baron." She exhaled a ragged breath. "I'm being silly."

"I do not think you are silly."

"I don't even know if these are actual memories. Or just something my mind has made up. It's so frustrating, like they're just out of reach."

But the present was right here, right now staring her in the face. And listening politely. She'd almost kissed him. And she wasn't at all sure she was free to make that kind of mistake.

He must have realized it, too, because he recovered his composure without advancing farther.

She busied herself by rummaging through his gym bag for shirt and pants, then stepped behind the canvas to change. She put on the oversize men's white shirt and tucked it into men's khaki pants that fit tight across the hips, but were loose in the waist and long in the leg.

Once she'd rolled up sleeves and pant legs, she felt reasonably dressed and much more composed herself. She could tell by the smile on Asad's face he still thought her bold for dressing like a man. Smiling back, she added the *bourque* and the vest with her holstered weapon for good measure.

"Go—" he nodded toward the watering hole "—while I take my turn."

Strolling toward the oasis, she freed the chain with the dog tags from the shirt. One thing she knew for sure. She *was* somebody's daughter. And quite possibly somebody's fiancée.

Wasn't it better to be somebody than nobody?

But who *was* she?

She'd barely stepped foot on the little patch of green surrounding the watering hole when she heard the putter of a small-engine, single-prop plane. Shading her eyes from the sun, she back-tracked toward Asad.

"Cessna Skyhawk," she made the offhand comment in passing. She continued to watch the plane, growing increasingly agitated as it circled over-head. "He's going to land!"

Her heart beat wildly to match the pounding in her ears.

She made a mad dash for the dune buggy. They were coming to get her. To take her back. And she had to stop them. She didn't want to lose her new-found freedom.

"Kalilah!" Asad shouted after her, followed by orders to his men.

By the time she realized he'd followed her with no thought to his modesty, she was already in the buggy racing toward the plane.

ZACH LOOKED UP from tying down the Cessna Skyhawk to the ground stakes. A dune buggy, kicking up a cloud of dust with the velocity of a sand storm, raced toward him. Followed in the distance by a Hummer.

His welcoming party.

Though he wasn't at all sure what to expect, Chaplain Matin had tried to assure him that the al Ra'id were a peaceful people. The desert itself extracted a high toll on human life. By nature and necessity, Bedouin were hospitable to strangers. The price of offending the dignity of man or tribe, on the other hand, was revenge by death. Lesser crimes or disputes were settled by a judge, usually the sheik, whose decision was absolute.

In other words, Zach had to hope he didn't offend anybody. Is that what had happened to McKenna's two agents—the ones who'd never returned from the desert?

He knew he didn't have the element of surprise coming in by plane, but his ability to keep his cool in the cockpit was something he trusted. He'd stood firm with McKenna. If he was going in unarmed, he was going in and coming out on his own terms. And that meant by plane.

McKenna had conceded the point with a private plane waiting for him in Riyadh, the capital of Saudi Arabia. Zach had insisted it be a Skyhawk, like the one he owned, so he didn't have to waste a moment of time learning a new instrument panel.

He tugged on the nylon cord one more time to make sure the knot would hold, but also to make sure he'd left enough slack for movement in case of high winds.

The dune buggy skidded to a halt a few feet away and he turned.

Michelle leaped from the driver's side.

And his heart damn near leaped to his throat. She looked thin enough to be blown away by a strong gust. Cheeks sunken. Eyes hollow and smudged with half moons beneath.

A bandage on her forehead.

Zach took one, two steps closer. He wanted to reassure himself that she was real. He wanted to wrap his arms around her and never let go.

"Feet apart. Hands against the plane!" she ordered, gun drawn.

"What the hell?" He saw absolutely no recognition in her eyes. *Was* she the terrorist McKenna claimed she'd become?

"Mouth shut. Do as you're told."

He raised his hands slowly, his mind going over every detail he could recall of Dr. Trahern's briefing on combat fatigue, post-traumatic stress disorder and transference, Stockholm syndrome. He turned around without a word and put his hands against the fuselage of the plane.

She tucked the gun somewhere and patted down his outstretched arms. His shoulders. As soon as she'd put the gun away, he could have easily overpowered her. But he didn't want to spook her, so he took it all in stride.

She felt her way around his chest from front to back and front again. His heart skipped a beat when he saw that she was wearing his ring. Mesmerized, he followed the path of her hands as they trailed down the outside of his legs.

And up the inside.

She cupped his balls. He jumped.

"Not so rough, sweetheart," he said over his shoulder. "But it's nice to see you, too."

She hesitated. Look confused. Met his eyes for the first time. Still no recognition.

"I've never seen you before in my life. Turn around. State your business," she demanded, the gun back in her hand and leveled at his heart.

Zach stared into Michelle's eyes for what seemed like an eternity. "Don't you recognize me?" he asked.

Before she could answer, the brand-new black Hummer rolled to a stop a few yards away. Four Arabs hopped out, two on either side, the three passengers heavily armed. Zach instinctively moved to put himself between Michelle and the heady-duty artillery.

"Kalilah! Are you all right?" The driver rushed toward them. "Don't be alarmed," he said to Zach by way of greeting. "She pulled a gun on me, too, when we first met."

Holstering her weapon, she said, "He's unarmed."

"Michelle?"

"I'm afraid you're mistaken," she denied. But he'd seen the flash of recognition at the name. "My name is Kalilah al Ra'id."

"Your name is Michelle Dann. And I'm the guy that goes with that ring."

CHAPTER SEVEN

RUB'AL-KHALI,
Arabian Desert

MICHELLE'S KNEES buckled and Zach caught her in a dead faint. Cradling her in his arms, he gently lowered her limp body to the sand.

"Michelle," he called to her, patted her pale face. "Wake up."

"She's been under a great deal of stress…" The driver of the black Hummer stood guard over them. His men stayed clear, weapons at their sides.

"I have some smelling salts." Zach nodded toward the plane. "In the first-aid kit. Under the seat." He raised his voice to be heard by the men rummaging through his plane.

It concerned Zach that Michelle wasn't coming around. He noticed the bump on her forehead, the bandage, which he removed to further examine the injury. It looked superficial and didn't extend into her scalp.

His Rapunzel had cut her hair.

He ran his fingers through her shorn locks, missing the length. But not one-tenth as much as he'd missed her. She moaned.

"Michelle? Can you hear me?"

She continued to groan in response.

"Kalilah?" The other man held the stick of smelling salts under her nose.

She shook her head from side to side, trying to shake the ammonia scent, but her lashes fluttered and she opened her eyes.

Zach stared down into their brown and barren depths, endless like the desert. No hint of recognition. But he couldn't even begin to describe the joy at seeing her again. In finding her alive. "Hi," he said simply. "Remember me now?"

She shook her head and straightened into a sitting position. Pulling away from him, she reached out to the man with the smelling salts and he helped her to her feet. "How are you feeling, Kalilah?"

"Her *name* is Michelle Dann."

"We suspected as much," the man she'd called Asad answered.

"I'm fine," she answered, calling a halt to their standoff.

"You have a bump on your head. You don't know who you are. And you don't know who I am. I'd say you're not fine," Zach stated flatly.

"She's suffering from amnesia."

Zach pulled himself up to his full height. "Is that what you call it?"

"I am no expert, of course."

"All the more reason to get her to a hospital."

"I'm not going anywhere," she said, backing away from him. "Asad?" She looked to the other man for guidance.

Zach stood, slack-jawed. The Michelle Dann he knew didn't let men stand around talking about her in the third person or look to a man to make her decisions. About the only thing that rang true was her refusal to let him take her to the hospital.

Asad addressed his men in Arabic. And Michelle headed off with them toward the Hummer. Zach moved in that direction.

"She is getting stronger every day. Come, let us get out of this heat."

LIKE A CAGED TIGER, Michelle prowled the length of Asad's tent. She turned toward the flap. Asad entered. She stopped.

"He's come to take you home, Kalilah. Michelle," Asad corrected.

"I know." She looked down at her hands. According to a stranger, she was Michelle Dann. U.S. Navy fighter pilot fallen to earth.

"You are afraid of him?" Asad asked.

She twisted her hands. "Yes. No. I don't know." She resumed her pacing. "I mean, he knows me. And I don't recognize him at all. That frightens me. What if…" She looked down at the ring. "What if he's lying?"

"You do not trust him?"

"At this point I don't trust anyone. Not even myself." She noticed the hurt in Asad's eyes and amended her statement. "Except maybe you, Asad. I trust you. If you think I should listen to him, I will."

"What I think is not important. But if this man holds the key to your past, you owe it to yourself to speak with him. I will not leave you alone with him unless you wish it."

She nodded.

Asad's man posted outside the tent let the stranger in. The stranger ducked his head to pass through the parted tent flap. His body followed. Tall, lean, well-muscled. From what he'd told her, a fighter pilot like herself. He wore desert-print fatigues—BDU, battle-dress uniform, he called it. He didn't look much like a pilot. He looked like a soldier.

If he was her fiancé how come she couldn't remember him?

A smile played at the corner of his mouth when he addressed her, "Hello again, Michelle."

She nodded. Stretched an uneasy smile across her face. And twisted the man's ring on her finger. They were using her name enough to make her sick of it. Trying to get her used to it, she supposed.

"Sweetheart, I'm here to take you home."

She stiffened. Sweetheart, darling. *Kalilah.* It had felt so natural. "Do you always call me that?" she ventured.

"Sweetheart? Yeah," he admitted. "But you don't like it much," he added.

"Then why—"

"I like it."

She continued to stare at him, processing this new information but unable to connect it to her past.

"I'll stop," he said, following her long silence.

He looked big and awkward standing there. But sincere. She turned to Asad for reassurance. He gestured that they should sit. And the three of them took seats on the floor of the tent.

"I'll listen to what you have to say," she said. "But I'm not willing to leave here with you just yet."

"Kalilah has asked me to negotiate her departure. She'd like some time to get used to the idea."

"How much time?"

"In three days' time we are hosting a gathering of tribes," Asad told him. "There will be feasting and celebration. Weddings. Camel races. Kalilah would like to stay for the festivities. And we would like the opportunity to say goodbye. Even though we have known her only a short time.'' Asad looked at her as he said this. She'd felt safe for such a very short time. Surly three days wasn't too much to ask. She turned to face the stranger.

''Fair enough,'' he said, leaning back against their host's pillows and making himself comfortable. Then to her, ''Why didn't you just ask me yourself?''

''Kalilah is wary of strangers,'' Asad answered.

''What did you say your name was?'' She managed to find her voice.

''Zach. Zach Prince.'' He smiled, and it was brighter than the Arabian sun. Even if she couldn't remember, she could see why she might have fallen in love with him.

Raja brought them coffee. Michelle poured a cup for their guest and tasted it. ''El-Heif,'' she said, topping off the cup. ''Now you taste. El-Keif, second cup.''

He did, looking at her over the brim of the mug with his sky-blue eyes. Something fluttered in her stomach.

Awareness?

He held out the cup. ''El-Dheif, cup of the guest,'' he said.

"You know the custom?" She poured a third time, filling the cup to the brim. Then she filled a cup for Asad and finally one for herself.

"How long have you been here?" he asked without answering her question.

Again Asad answered for her. "Not very long."

Zach Prince kept his gaze locked with hers.

"How long have I been gone?"

"A month," he answered.

"Where have you been?" she asked.

She expected him to say, "Looking for you." Instead, he stared into his half-full mug and set it aside before meeting at gaze once more.

"I thought you were dead, Michelle. I can't begin to tell you how happy I am that you're not. Or how sorry I am—"

"Sorry? For what?"

His gaze shifted to Asad.

She hugged her knees to her chest and waited for Zach's answer.

"There's so much we have to say to each other. But later. When you're safe at home. Your mom and dad are worried sick—"

"You haven't satisfied my curiosity yet. I have many more questions before we leave." She sighed. "I'm tired." She rested her aching head against her knees.

"It's the heat." Asad pushed to his feet and

helped her to hers. "I'll have Raja move your things to her tent," Asad said. "Your *friend* can stay here with me."

Zach looked ready to protest as he rose to his feet. Raja, who'd been quietly hovering in the background since bringing them their coffee, began gathering Michelle's few things from around the tent.

The two men sized each other up. Michelle could almost see their chests puff and their shoulders square. And whatever imaginary string it was that pulled them to their full heights.

Suddenly she felt very irritated with them both. Asad had purposely led the man who was supposed to be her fiancé to believe that she and Asad were sharing a tent. Which they were. But not in *that* way.

And Zach had walked in here assuming he could call her sweetheart and she'd go with him wherever it was he'd wanted to take her.

She stormed past them both, her irritation increasing with each step. She told herself it was just the desert heat.

ZACH WATCHED Michelle stalk away. If Asad was to be believed, she had amnesia. And had only been here a short time. That would explain a few things. Like why she didn't recognize him at all.

But it wouldn't explain why she'd cozy up to one man while wearing another man's ring.

"You cannot force her to go with you. Three days is not so very long," Asad said.

"I suppose you'd like her to stay?"

"Kalilah is good company. But I am a simple man with a simple life. And I would not force a complicated woman from fulfilling her destiny."

I'll just bet. It was on the tip of Zach's tongue to say it out loud. But it wouldn't do to insult his host. And then there was McKenna's theory that she was a pawn. In what game? And who controlled her?

The leader of the al Ra'id? This man, Khahn Asad al Ra'id.

"I only want to make Michelle happy. That's all I've ever wanted."

"And if you are not that man? Can you make her fall in love with you a second time?"

"She's suffering a little shell shock, that's all. She'll come around."

"In your shoes I would attempt to gain her trust rather than regain lost memories."

"Thanks for the advice." Judging from the look on the man's face, Zach's sarcasm wasn't wasted on him.

"Amnesia can result in permanent memory loss. Even a personality change. She may never have a breakthrough. Then again, she may regain her lost memories all of a sudden or over time.''

''Excuse me, but you said you were no expert.''

''Internet access. We are not uncivilized.''

''Speaking of which, I'll want the things your men took from my plane.''

''Specifically, your cell phone and laptop computer?''

''Exactly.''

Three days later
CAMEL RACES

''THE CHILDREN SEEM to like him,'' Michelle commented to Raja from where they stood along the sidelines waiting for the camel races to begin. Several tribes in the area had gathered for the all-day event.

''That's because he gives them sweets.''

Both women watched as Zach Prince doled out more bubble gum to eager outstretched hands. The excited chatter and happy laughter had followed him through the camp the entire three days he'd been here.

''Khanh Asad has given your friend a camel to ride in the races. It is a great honor. Tonight there will be a feast to pay homage to the winners.''

''That man has about all the attention he needs.''

Michelle noted a few of the young women of the camp approaching him now for their taste of something sweet. There was no language barrier when it came to flirting.

"He is very strong and handsome," Raja said. "He will produce many fine sons."

"That doesn't mean he has to populate the whole camp." The subject of their discussion was showing off by blowing bubbles for the entertainment of three young women.

"I've made you angry? Forgive me for speaking of your betrothed in such a manner."

"We're not exactly..." Michelle started, then touched her ring finger with her thumb. She felt the precious metal. Solid and enduring. "I guess we are betrothed."

I pledge thee my troth. Faith, loyalty. Truth. Weren't those wedding vows?

"But you have feelings for Khanh Asad," Raja mumbled.

Michelle looked at the other woman. Head bowed, eyes on Khanh in the distance, where he examined the camels competing in the first heat.

"My feelings for Asad are simply gratitude, Raja. But I think you have a thing for the sheik."

"A thing?"

"The hots? He turns you on."

"Oh, yes. I lust after him." The young woman

blushed. "I am but an orphan with no male relatives to form an alliance with Khanh Asad. My mother died in childbirth and my father and brother were killed in raids by the al Mukhtar. Is your father a great man?"

Michelle reached for a memory of her father, but there was nothing there to hold on to. Zach would know. She'd have to ask him. He'd said her parents were worried. And several times he'd tried to talk her into leaving sooner. She felt a pang of guilt for not agreeing to do so.

But because she had no memory of her American home, she had no sense of it as a refuge. So she'd chosen to stay a little while longer. What if nowhere felt as safe as the desert?

"If your father is a great man," Raja continued, "you would have much to offer the al Ra'id."

"I'm sure my father is a very ordinary man," Michelle said. "And I'm sure Asad would be very happy to have someone who loves him as much as you obviously do."

"Do not forget lust," Raja teased, then spoiled the cheeky statement by blushing again.

"I happen to know Asad likes bold women," Michelle said to encourage the girl.

"Does your man like bold women?"

Raja asked the hardest questions. And the an-

swers could all be found in one place. "Excuse
me, Raja."

Michelle marched over to the bubble-gum ban-
dit. "Can I have a piece?"

"Of gum?"

"What else would I be talking about?" She
knew flirting when she heard it. But she wasn't
about to let him think she would give in to his
charm.

The smile spread across his face. He dug into
his shirt pocket of his BDU. "My last one," he
offered.

"Thank you." She unwrapped it. Read the joke.
"I don't get it."

"You never do. And since when do you chew
gum?"

"I don't chew gum?" Popping it into her mouth,
she flirted back.

He searched her face. "You do whatever the
heck you please. It's just so damn good to see you
again."

He made her uncomfortable when he talked like
that. And yet she wished she could say the same
thing. Feel the same thing. That it was good to see
him, too. "What do you see when you look at
me?"

"What? You mean hair color, eye color?"

"For that I can look in a mirror. But what do

you see?'' In his eyes she saw the sea and the sky. And something deeper, bluer. ''Do you love me? Lust for me? Why did you ask me to marry you?'' Did she sound a little bit desperate for the answer?

''Are you really ready to hear the truth?''

Yes. No. ''Just because you know and I don't doesn't mean you should only dole out information you think I'm ready to hear. How do I know you're even telling me the truth?''

The brim of his ball cap shaded his eyes. SEALs—was that supposed to mean something other than a sea mammal?

''I guess that's where trust comes into play,'' he said. ''But if you really trusted me, you'd leave here with me right now.''

''I can't.''

''I know.'' He sounded sad. ''And that's why I'm not going to answer your questions.''

''Now you're just pissing me off.''

''That should be familiar territory. We're leaving here tomorrow. Get used to the idea.'' He headed off in the direction of the camel racers.

A rifle shot rang out. Michelle jumped.

The first heat was off and running toward the finish line in a cloud of dust. Her heartbeat thundered along with the hoofbeats of the half-dozen or so racers. And she got caught up in the excitement of the moment with the rest of the spectators.

Even though she didn't have a favorite, she couldn't help but scream her encouragement to the underdog when the camel in second place moved up to take the lead. Only then did Raja point out that she was cheering for the wrong team.

Michelle paid closer attention to the tribal colors after that.

Several heats later, Zach and Asad lined up at the starting line. Michelle felt her own competitive spirit kick in. She didn't want to watch. She wanted to ride like the wind. Maybe she'd never known anything about being a camel jockey, but it was clear that Zach didn't, either. And that wasn't stopping him.

The men of the tribe were giving him a quick lesson on the ins and outs of camel racing. The shot sounded. He kicked his beast into high gear. Quick learner or fierce competitor, he managed to stay with the pack. As they thundered up the make-shift track, he ran neck and neck with Asad in third place.

The fact there were two riders ahead of them didn't seem to matter. They battled out third place. Each vying to take the lead from the other.

Dust kicked up all around them.

"Come on! Come on!" she shouted, not even sure who she was rooting for, Asad or Zach.

The camel in second place stumbled. The jockey

fell. Zach veered around the fallen rider, but tangled with the riderless animal. Michelle held her breath for what seemed like ages. He fell hard. Ate sand. But somehow managed to roll out of the way of the lag riders.

She missed the photo-finish ending—minus the photo. Several spectators gathered to congratulate the winners, but she ran toward the fallen man to see for herself that he was really all right.

Zach sat in the sand, arms draped over his knees. "I'm okay," he snapped before she could ask. "Nothing's hurt but my pride."

"And you're sitting on that." She smiled down at him.

She could tell he was trying not to smile. "Remind me not to get on one of those smelly beasts again."

"I'm sure I'll forget. I'm the one without the memory, remember?"

"I had him," he grumbled, ignoring her attempt at levity. "Any fool could see that."

"What was the side bet? Or were you two just trying to impress the girls?"

He looked up at her with that hurt-little-boy look. Her heart skipped a beat. "Oh, I see."

She tried not to laugh. But he took the loss way too seriously. "In case you didn't notice, the girl came running in your direction."

Zach reached out his hand to Michelle. She was right. Asad had won the race. But he was sitting here looking up at the girl. He'd never tried winning by losing before.

"Your sleeve's torn." She took his hand. "Oh, Zach," she scolded, getting her first look at the skin that felt like it had been sandblasted off the back of his forearm. "We're going to need to get you cleaned up."

"Nothing but a scrape," he said, hoisting himself to his feet, not an easy thing to do, since he felt as if he'd been run over by a truck. He didn't let go of her hand, though. And he didn't exactly mind her fussing over him. He only wished she'd let him fuss over her the same way.

She let go of his hand and led the way back to the encampment in the distance. The gathering crowd had started to drift back that way, also.

A group of older women were cooking over an open fire, preparing for the feast. A group of younger women were gathering around a small cottage built on a camel's back and chatting excitedly with the young woman inside.

"Oh, they're getting the bride ready to meet her groom," Michelle said in passing.

"They've never met?" Zach asked. "Does he know what he's getting himself into?"

"They've met. Fallen in love. And he's asked

for her hand. Now her family is going to deliver her on the back of the camel.''

"I guess the poor sucker knocked her up. And her family is dumping her off with the dowry. A simple enough ceremony.''

"If you're such a cynic when it comes to marriage, how did you ever manage to propose? Wait here. Asad keeps a first-aid kit in his tent. I won't be a minute.''

"I have one, too.''

She disappeared into the tent, then poked her head out moments later with a blue canvas tote. "This it?'' she asked.

"That's it.''

"You never answered my question. Or is that one of those questions you're not going to answer until I'm ready to hear the answer?''

"How come you don't ask me questions about your life? Where you grew up. Your home. Your parents.''

She poured water over his arm and he hissed in a sharp breath.

"I thought I *was* asking questions about my life.'' She dabbed his arm gently with swabbing. "Okay, I'll bite. When did we first meet?''

"Technically that's a *we* question. Not a *you* question. But I can answer that one. We first met in the nursery of the naval hospital in Pensacola,

Florida. Your mother delivered by C-section and six days later they were wheeling you out the door just as they were wheeling me in.''

"You don't remember back that far.''

"That's the way my mother tells it. My first memory of you, I was five. My dad was the CO of SEAL training. That's in Coronado, California. And your dad was coming on board as the executive officer. There's this big bell near the flagpole, next to the headquarters building. Your dad walked across the grinder with you in tow. He let go of your hand to shake hands with my dad. And you stuck your thumb in your mouth and hid behind his leg.''

Of course, while their dads were busy catching up, he'd talked her into ringing the bell and got them both in trouble. And he'd done all the talking. She hadn't said a word until they were leaving. Then she pulled out her thumb and said, "Bye, Zach, nice to meet you.''

"We've really known each other that long? And our dads were in the Navy?''

"Best friends. Since before we were born. My dad retired when I was about nine. Your dad is still in the Navy. He's an admiral. The chief of SEALs.''

"A pretty important man,'' she mumbled. "And we're in the Navy?''

"Yeah, still are."

"A family tradition?"

"I guess. You wanted to fly jets."

"And what did you want to do?"

"Fly jets."

"We get along pretty good, then, huh?"

"Match made in heaven." When she wasn't pissed off at him.

"And I was shot down…"

"A little over a month ago."

"And I can't remember anything before three days ago." She wrapped the bandage around his arm. "Do you know where I've been?"

"No." He shook his head. "Not before you came here."

She seemed to lose herself in thought then.

"Michelle." He lifted her chin and made her look into his eyes. "It doesn't matter to me where you've been. I just want you home."

She gently removed his hand. "It matters to me. And maybe it will matter to you. It must be something really horrible if I'm trying this hard to forget."

She left him, taking his first-aid kit with her, and headed off in the direction of the tent she shared with Raja.

CHAPTER EIGHT

Later that evening
THE WEDDING

"WHERE HAVE YOU BEEN?" Raja chided. "The wedding processional is about to begin."

It was on the tip of Michelle's tongue to tell the other woman she didn't want to go. But that would be impolite. "What are we waiting for?"

"Would you like to borrow some clothes to change into?"

"I'm fine."

Raja sighed, telling her she didn't look fine in her opinion.

"I'm comfortable," she amended. Too comfortable to want to leave. Too miserable to stay.

Ever since Zach had shown up, her cocoon was no longer that satisfying.

Heading for the crowd gathering in the distance, they joined the slow-moving processional. The bright orange ball dipped low in the west. The dividing line between night and day melded in hues of orange and blue. It would be dark soon. The soft baying of the camels mixed with song.

Time for the wedding feast.

Time for the honeymoon.

Zach had avoided answering her question about why he'd proposed. What was he keeping from her? Or rather, what hadn't she asked that needed asking?

Despite his claims that her missing past didn't matter, how would it really affect their future?

Michelle moved along with the rest of the young women in the tribe, well behind the bride's family and apart from the gaiety all around her. The joining of the bride and groom passed by in a blur, as did most of the wedding feast of *mensaf,* a traditional rice dish made with yogurt and served with lamb or beef.

She wasn't very hungry. And it was okay to cry at weddings. Even Bedouin weddings. Because no one seemed to notice her misery. Not even Asad.

And especially not Zach.

He'd disappeared from the spot where she'd left him. Asad sat in judgment inside his tent, settling disputes among fellow tribesmen or in some cases between al Ra'id tribesmen and visiting clan.

Gathered around the fires outside, his men were in conversation, sometimes heated debate. And the name that came up most often was the al Mukhtar.

A shiver raced up her spine.

She gathered the *bourque* around her shoulders and went in search of something warmer to take the chill off the night.

Commander's Moon

ZACH STEERED CLEAR of the festivities. The guards passed a time or two, but left him alone unchallenged. He leaned against the hood of the Hummer, listening to the bay of a camel, feeling the bone-cold chill of the desert at night.

Pilots knew meteorology.

Zach had come prepared for the hundred-and-twenty-five degree heat of day to give way to the forty-degree cold at night.

In the desert, rainfall amounted to less than ten inches a year. Without moisture there were no clouds. Heat escaped at night. And beat down during the day.

His bomber jacket, along with the rest of his belongings, was in Asad's tent, and Zach didn't feel like breaking the peace and quiet of his own thoughts to go get it just yet. Of course, his thoughts weren't exactly peaceful or quiet. More like a riot of turmoil.

He was back to wondering just how much Michelle remembered. She'd as much as admitted that the memory of her captivity was so horrible she'd rather forget. So was it really forgotten? Or just pushed aside where she wouldn't have to deal with it. Was he being truthful with her, with himself, when he said the past didn't matter?

Her captivity didn't matter.

It sure as hell mattered when he saw her hovering around Asad's tent all evening. Waiting for the man to finish up his business? Asad had only moved her out of his tent a few days ago. Maybe they were starting to miss each other. Zach had been doing without sleep to make sure something clandestine wasn't going on.

How would he feel if Asad's arms was where she chose to spend tonight? It was the same question he'd asked himself every night for the past three nights. He ran a hand through his hair. He knew he wouldn't be able to stand by and watch it happen.

Then he'd been lying to Asad when he'd said he only wanted to make Michelle happy.

Thank God they were leaving tomorrow.

But what if he wasn't the man who could make her happy? Then he'd have a hard time explaining to McKenna how he started a war over one woman. Because he wasn't just going to let Asad take her.

His wingman. His woman.

She wasn't dead, but was she still his?

Zach watched as Michelle made her way from the noisy crowds near Asad's tent to the deserted end of the camp near her own quarters. She stopped to exchange a few words with Raja. The women hugged.

Funny, he'd never thought of her as the kind of woman who had much use for girlfriends. He'd never seen her hug Skeeter. Nor had he ever overheard them talking about anything except jets.

And that was the real kicker. He could understand her forgetting him. But jets? Somebody must have really done a number on her head. It was up to him to bring her back.

Michelle ducked into her tent. He let out the breath he'd been holding. Maybe he wouldn't get any sleep tonight. But he could feel the tension slipping away just knowing that Asad wouldn't be getting anything else.

But then she reappeared a few minutes later with her flight suit on. He straightened, on full alert. He didn't like seeing her in the bloodstained clothes. But he suspected she'd put them on over the other outfit to ward off the chill.

He held his breath, waiting for her next move, but she clung to the shadows by her tent.

Zach made his way back to camp, back to Michelle, guided by the light of the full moon, but sticking to the shadows whenever possible. Well after 0200 hours, and the party showed no signs of breaking up.

He reached her tent. Watched her watching Asad. Longing evident in her beautiful moonlit face.

Zach felt the dagger plunge straight to his heart.

Across the campfire Raja whispered in Asad's ear, then danced away toward the Bedouin sheik's tent. Asad got up and followed her.

Zach didn't know whether to feel sorry for Michelle. Or a little smug satisfaction for himself.

He stepped up behind her.

"Maybe it'll be your turn tomorrow night. Oops, I forgot we'll be gone." He could have bitten off his tongue as soon as he said it.

"Oh, grow up, Zach," she said without turning around. "Remind me again why we got engaged when you can be such a jerk."

"What you see is what you get. Why don't you tell me?"

She turned to face him, folding her arms. "There must be an awful lot of pain behind those smart-ass comments of yours. I don't remember a thing about you, yet I have a feeling I'm seeing you clearly for the very first time."

"*You're* the one who walks around with a chip on her shoulder."

"Ah, so now the gloves come off. We're going home tomorrow and you don't feel you have to try so hard around me anymore. I have a chip? I have news for you—all my problems have been wiped away. It's a clean slate."

"News flash. Your problems still exist whether you remember them or not!"

"Are you one of my problems? I wasn't wearing this ring three days ago. Maybe we'd already broken if off. Do you think you're doing me some big favor by not telling me we hate each other? Because I would really like to know. You know what. Let's not even wait for tomorrow. I'm ready to leave right now." She stormed into her tent.

"And for your information, hotshot—" she turned, holding back the flap "—I wasn't standing here daydreaming about Asad. Romantic fool that I apparently am, I was wishing I could remember what falling in love was like. If I could get one memory back, the day you proposed is the one I want." She let the flap drop, silent, but as effective as any slamming door.

But not as secure.

He didn't even let her start tying down the flaps before he pushed his way in.

"What do you think you're doing?"

He cleared his throat. "We're not engaged. The day you were shot down, you carried that ring with you in the cargo pocket of your flight suit, but you never knew it. And I never got an answer."

She stared at her ring finger.

"What do you think my answer would have been?"

"I think we were better friends than lovers. And I think you would have told me to go straight to hell. So don't rack your brain trying to remember falling in love with me 'cause maybe that one just ain't there."

Tears started welling in her eyes.

"How did you propose?"

"I put the ring in a piece of gum, wrapped it back up and gave it to you." His voice turned from matter-of-fact to serious. "I had erased the comic and penciled 'Marry me' in the balloon. But I thought maybe if your answer was no, you'd play it off as a joke…"

"That sounds sweet." She sniffled. "Except the part about the joke. What if I thought you were the one who wasn't serious?"

He shrugged. "I'd asked once before. You said no." He looked uncomfortable. "You need help packing your things?"

"Were we really lousy lovers?"

"Just inexperienced. It was a long time ago."

"Were you my first?"

"Yeah."

"Was I your first?"

"Yeah."

"What if I wanted you to make love to me now?"

He opened his mouth. Only air came out.

"I take it that's not something the Michelle you know would say. Then maybe you don't know me as well as you think you do, 'cause I'm the one saying it. And I think I would have said yes to that proposal."

"You're not acting like yourself. I'm not going to take advantage of you when you're like this."

She reached for his belt and pulled him closer. "Don't you know it's every woman's fantasy to make love to a stranger?"

"No. At least, I didn't know it was yours."

"If you have a problem with *your* Michelle acting this way, you can call me sweetheart or darling." She unclasped his belt. "Or Kalilah."

With one pull, she yanked his belt free from the loops.

"You're two fantasies for the price of one. It's not every day a girl gets a second first time with the stranger she's known all her life." She brought his face down to hers. "I reserve the right to give you my answer to your proposal when I know what it is. And when I remember falling in love with you, I'll tell you. Now you'd better kiss me or I'm going to feel really stupid.''

Zach lowered his mouth to hers.

"Say my name," she murmured.

"Kalilah," he managed through parched lips.

"Every year on our anniversary you can be the tall dark stranger who came to the Bedouin camp and I'll be your Arab slave girl. My answer is *yes.*"

"Michelle." In his hunger to have her, he devoured her mouth. In his thirst to quench her every desire, he rained kisses on her face. "I want you so bad."

She undid the buttons of his shirt, pushed it off his shoulders, trapping his arms so that she could be the aggressor once again.

She ran her hands over the hard planes of his chest. Across his nipples. He moaned. She pushed him back onto the sheepskins. Fell on top of him.

"Do I like it on top?" she asked.

"Oh, yes," he groaned.

Then he caught a glimpse of the scared little slave girl in her eyes. Knew she desperately wanted to make a connection. Feel something real and maybe out of reach.

He slowed them down to a leisurely stroll through the garden of pleasure. Kissed her slowly. Gently. Tenderly.

Ever mindful that at any moment this all might come to a screeching halt. Lord help him. He didn't want it to stop.

His shirt fell by the wayside. And he rolled her beneath him. Hand poised at the zipper of her flight suit, he asked, "What's my name?"

"Zach," she said on a sigh.

He trailed the zipper past her navel.

"When did we first meet?"

"In the nursery... By the bell," she answered between breathless kisses. "Today... Yesterday..."

"Close enough." He freed the buttons of her shirt. She wasn't wearing a bra and he cupped her bare breast.

"Oh," she breathed.

"When did we first make love?" He teased her nipple to a hardened peak.

"Now." She writhed beneath him. "When we were virgins." She let out a groan.

He lowered his head and closed his mouth over her flesh. He raised his head to look into her eyes. "When did we fall in love?" He touched her wet nipple. Trailed his hand along the same path as the zipper, past her flat belly. He slipped his hand between her thighs.

She was slick. And hot. And ready for him.

He touched her as if she were the most delicate desert blossom.

"Ah," she moaned, closing her eyes.

"When did we fall in love?" he repeated, desperately needing to hear that she loved him.

"I'm...still...falling," she panted.

He smiled at her answer. "Open your eyes, Michelle. Say my name."

"Zach," she panted out his name over and over again. He took her to new heights, using the stars in her eyes to guide him.

"I'm still falling, too. And we're just getting started."

He stripped the oversize flight suit from her. Struggled with the clothes underneath until she lay bare before his hungry eyes.

Then he trailed his lips down her body, culminating in a most intimate kiss.

Michelle's world exploded, and she couldn't deny she was his. She pulled him up from between her thighs by gripping fistfuls of his short jet-black hair. And she seared his mouth in a kiss so hot he'd never doubt he was hers.

"Zach, I want you inside me," she demanded.

"Sweetheart, we don't have a condom."

"In your first-aid kit we do." She smiled up at him, reaching for the blue canvas bag.

"Are you sure? Maybe this isn't such a good

idea.'' She handed the condom to him. "But then again, who am I to argue?'' he said, taking the package. "Wrap your legs around me, sweetheart. We're going for a ride.''

She gave him a playful smack upside the head.

And he got serious. "I thought I lost you on the way to heaven.'' He leaned in and kissed her so thoroughly he could have deprived her brain of oxygen and she'd have kept on kissing him until she passed out or died happy. They made love slowly, then made love again in the fevered pitch of two hot sweaty bodies deprived too long of sustenance.

Near dawn they began to make love for a third time, and he reached for another condom package.

She snagged his wrist. "I want to make a baby with you.'' She barely held her desperation in check. "Now, tonight.''

He went completely still. "You can't get pregnant. You're on birth control. The five-year plan.''

He moved from their bed so fast the chill night replaced his body heat before she even realized the consequences of what she'd said. Of course, she'd forgotten. She touched the underside of her arm. Norplant.

They were using condoms for another reason. She had no memory of the past month, which meant she didn't remember who she'd been with.

She felt dirty and ashamed.

"I'm sorry," she said stiffly. "I shouldn't have even suggested—"

"No need to apologize, Michelle." His voice cracked.

"I'd probably wind up giving you some kind of horrible disease."

"I wasn't even thinking about that." He stood facing the tent. "We already made a baby once. We were seventeen."

"What do you mean?"

"You wanted to go to the naval academy. You wanted to be a fighter pilot. You couldn't do that married or pregnant."

"I did not do what you are suggesting!" She knelt on the bed and pressed a hand to her stomach.

"I don't know what you did." He took a deep breath. "I wasn't part of the decision. But I can't blame you for not wanting to marry a guy you thought would be flipping burgers the rest of his life to support you. I tried to convince you it wouldn't be that bad. But you were probably right. You're pretty much always right." He sniffed. And kept his back to her. "God, I haven't thought about that in a long time. I guess something you don't want to contemplate is easy to push from your mind."

"You're a liar! Get out!" She threw his pants

at him. "I never want to see you again as long as I live. I would never do that!"

"I'm sorry I wasn't man enough for you, Michelle," he said, stepping into his pants.

Firecrackers popped somewhere outside the tent.

Horses nickered and whinnied. More firecrackers.

And screams.

"Stay down," he ordered. Grabbing her weapons, he went outside to investigate.

Michelle scrambled into Zach's discarded shirt and followed.

Dawn streaked the sky. The ground vibrated under pounding hooves. Raiders mounted on horseback rode through the camp, setting tents on fire.

Clouds of billowing smoke choked out visibility.

Shots awaited the unwary running from the flames and into the sights of the raiders' poised weapons. If they were lucky enough to escape being trampled beneath the powerful horses.

Women and children screamed.

Asad shouted orders. Men took up arms and fired back. Blood flowed.

Much as it did the day she'd arrived.

Michelle stood at the entrance of her tent, shaking.

"Get down!" Zach slammed her body to the ground. Rolled them out of the way of a rider.

He poised to fire on the retreating back of the cowards who'd left a path of destruction in their wake. Until he realized most or all of them carried off women.

Then all went quiet. Eerily quite.

"RAJA! RAJA!" Michelle screamed, leaping to her feet. She raced toward the fallen woman.

Zach followed and caught her. Surveying the destruction, he pulled her closer.

"She's dead," he said. He'd seen her shot, then trampled. Blood pooled around her head. He tucked Michelle into the safety of his arms and tried to shield her from the sight.

But Michelle broke free and covered the remaining few feet to her friend's body. She dropped to the ground and cradled the dead woman in her arms. "Raja. Oh, Raja." Michelle rocked back and forth. "Don't die on me now, Sara! Oh, Sara!"

"Michelle?" Zach queried softly. His Michelle.

She looked up at him with tears streaking her beautiful face. "Skeeter's dead."

"I know."

"I tried to stop her. But she killed herself. She was hurt during ejection. She knew I wouldn't leave her. And she killed herself to save me." She looked down at Raja's body, then back up at Zach. "They were after me, weren't they."

He didn't answer, just reached down and pulled Michelle to her feet.

Asad stumbled toward them, coughing from smoke inhalation. "We ride on the al Mukhtar tonight."

"I'm going with you," Zach said.

"You can't leave me!" Michelle cried.

He looked into her eyes. "You're right. I can't." And she was right about the raiders' purpose. "They killed Raja as she was coming out of your tent," he said to Asad, hoping the man would understand what he was trying to say without his having to spell it out. "And they rode off with a half dozen women."

The riders had been after only one woman.

CHAPTER NINE

THEY DROVE in silence. Fire had destroyed the al Ra'id camp and with it, their few possessions. They'd managed to save a couple of items from Michelle's tent, but the loss of Zach's cell phone and lap top computer, as well as Asad's, meant they were well and truly cut off from the outside world.

Their only chance was to reach the Cessna.

Michelle shivered. She kept thinking about the injured Asad and their abrupt departure. She would have liked the chance to…what?…say goodbye, thank him, make amends? But Zach had spirited her away.

Someone wanted her dead.

Both Zach and Asad knew it, too, but they weren't giving her the full story. Asad's people were better off without her around.

Is your father a great man? Raja's question

came back to haunt her. Her father was a very great man with five thousand Navy SEALs at his disposal. Was someone using her as a pawn? For what purpose?

As the sun rose higher in the sky she got her first chance to really study Zach's profile. She couldn't decipher the stern expression.

Did he blame her for the destruction? For ending a pregnancy that never existed? Oh, yes, she'd gotten all her memories back. Even the bittersweet ones.

Still as they raced toward the Cessna, she knew Zach was the one person in this godforsaken desert she could trust with her life. And that trust was tested before they could reach the plane. They were five hundred yards away when it exploded into a ball of flames.

From the west, a horse and rider wearing the robes of the al Makhtar thundered toward them at full speed. As he neared, he fired.

"Head down." Zach ordered, pushing her head toward his lap. He zigged and zagged to dodge the flying bullets, but the rider pulled even. Aimed his gun at her. Zach steered hard left and the dune buggy pitched and rolled down a dune.

They used the overturned vehicle for cover as Zach shot at their assailant. The horse reared, throwing its rider, before galloping off. After several minutes in which the rider did nothing but lie in the sand, Zach got to his feet.

"What if he's faking it?" She tried to pull him back down.

"That's what I have to find out."

He kept low, his weapon drawn. He reached the body. Recognized the prone figure. "McKenna?" he said.

The man raised his gun. Fired. Zach leaped away.

Michelle fired. Once. Twice. Dead on target.

The man, McKenna, dropped back to the sand, and Zach kicked his gun aside.

McKenna coughed and sputtered. Blood seeped from the corner of his mouth. He laughed, a bitter wheeze of a sound. "They shoot down our jets. They kill our pilots and we do nothing but talk." McKenna laughed. "They should have killed her. Her life wasn't worth anything anyway. Just like my brother's life wasn't worth anything when he was shot down." He coughed again. "She was my Helen of Troy. But she escaped. My plan still would have worked. If the al Ra'id had finished the job. We would have been drawn into war. But the al Ra'id is weak! Mitch is weak. You're all weak."

"You're the one who's weak," Michelle said.

"You brought only shame to your brother's sac-rifice."

AFTER THEY BURIED McKenna, they righted the buggy and managed to get it going again. They'd have to find another way to escape now that the plane was destroyed. It was while they were driving that she noticed for the first time the rip in Zach's sleeve.

"You're hurt," she said, reaching for his arm.

He shrugged off her touch. She pulled back.

The dune buggy began to slow, then roll. "Come on, come on." Zach tapped the gas pedal. The vehicle stopped.

"Out of gas?" she queried.

"Yeah." Zach put his head against the steering wheel. "Just my luck."

He hopped out and unhooked a five-gallon gas can from the back of the buggy. "Dry as a bone," he said, tossing the damaged can aside. Muscling their gear, he started to walk. "According to the map, we're about six miles from the nearest air-port, which happens to be in Iraq."

Michelle sat in the disabled buggy. "I'm not going back there." She stared at him, heart pound-ing in her chest.

"We have no way of getting in touch with any-one. We need to make it out on our own."

Michelle turned and looked in the direction from which they'd come. When she turned back their eyes met.

Zach cursed under his breath. Then he walked the few steps back to her. He tipped his head. She got out and started walking. They followed the sandy road in single file well into the afternoon. Zach came even with her once to offer his canteen. She took a long pull and would have had a second, but he tugged it away.

"That's enough for now," he said without taking a drink himself.

The next time he offered she took one cautious sip, stopping when she dribbled, wanting to save every drop. She wiped her mouth with the back of her hand. This time she made sure Zach took a drink.

She wished he'd say something to her.

Her dreams of this day, of seeing him again, shattered with the reality. She sighed and stepped back in line. By the time they'd walked a few more miles in the scorching sun, Michelle could barely manage to put one foot in front of the other.

"You're not going to make it much farther," he said. How he knew that without once looking back at her, Michelle didn't know. He stopped and checked his watch. "Why don't we rest and wait out this heat."

They hiked together to the spot he'd indicated. He set up a lean-to for shade, then started digging in the sand with his bare hands. Michelle was left to feel useless.

"Why don't you get out of the sun?" he suggested.

She moved to sit in the lean-to.

"Are you taking me home?" she asked in a lost voice, still disoriented by the turn of events.

"Yes." He nodded reassuringly.

She let out a breath that she seemed to have been holding forever. And took several more deep cleansing ones. Tears formed at the corners of her gritty eyes and she swiped at them.

"What are you doing?" She attempted a conversation.

"Digging a well."

"A what?"

He had dug down about two feet in a four-by-four square hole, then dug out another round hole in the center. He cut off the top of an empty water bottle and placed it in the middle of the hole. Then he climbed out and placed a clear plastic sheet over the whole thing.

After securing the four corners with rocks, he placed a small rock in the center. He stood back to admire his handiwork as Michelle admired the hard planes of his body.

God, she'd missed him. Last night they'd made love and this morning they were strangers again.

"It creates a greenhouse effect," he explained. "Condensation forms and drips toward the bottle."

"I remember. From survival training. Rest at night. Replenish during the day. Only I didn't have any plastic."

She wrapped her arms around her knees and rested her chin on top, watching Zach as he began working on another well. She sighed heavily. He was hurting more than he was letting on.

She reached for the first aid kit. "Zach, would you please stop so I can have a look at your arm?"

"We need two wells."

"I'll finish the next one," she offered.

Zach stood and brushed the sand from his hands, but didn't move to sit beside her. Michelle got up and went to him.

"Let me have a look at your arm."

"It's just a scratch."

"Even scratches can get infected." She picked at the hole in his sleeve, deciding whether to rip it or have him take off his shirt.

He didn't shrug her off this time, but he seemed indifferent to her touch.

"Let's do this in the shade."

He snorted, but complied, ducking inside the

lean-to. She sat down on the side of his injured arm.

"Do you need help getting your shirt off?" she asked, thinking to prompt him into making an effort.

He just turned and stared at her with challenge in his eyes.

She reached in with one hand and opened his first button. He seemed intent on making her do all the work. She had to use two hands in order to untuck his T-shirt.

She felt his stomach muscles tense, but he watched her in silence. "Let me know if I'm hurting you," she said.

"Ouch," he said sarcastically, even though she'd done no more than unbutton his shirt. But there was something behind the look in his eyes that told her she'd hurt him.

"We need to talk about the baby," she said.

"There's a whole lot we need to talk about, but we need to get the hell out of here first."

The desert-print fatigues looked like those her dad used to wear. She slipped the material past his shoulders, careful of his injured arm. She'd forgotten to undo the buttons at his cuffs and had to work at them to free his arms.

Dried blood kept the T-shirt beneath stuck to the wound. She didn't want to just peel off the shirt and start it bleeding again. So she opened up the first-aid kit to see what she could use. She dabbed at the injury with one of the premoistened towelettes. When that didn't work, she moistened the T-shirt directly with water from his canteen.

Even that started him bleeding again.

She stanched the flow with gauze. The arm was much worse than she'd first suspected. Fortunately the bullet had passed through the meaty part of his shoulder, missing the bone.

"We should have stopped and taken care of this earlier."

"I'll live. In spite of you."

"What's that supposed to mean?"

"You tell me."

She sat back on her heels. "I don't know what you're talking about."

"You might try."

"What in hell has happened to you?" She stunned him into silence. She wanted to apologize, make him understand. "You said you didn't want to talk about the baby right now."

"I don't!"

He stalked away. She stumbled to her feet.

"I waited for you!" she screamed. "I waited. But you never came." She turned her back on him, not knowing what to do with her anger or her tears.

It was all out in the open now. The baby. The blame. The botched elopement.

When Michelle mustered the courage to turn back around, she could see Zach sitting in the distance, hat pulled down over his eyes. She took a few steps in the same direction, then turned her attention and frustration on digging the second well.

When she finished, she kept her hands busy by tidying up the first-aid kit. She'd never dressed Zach's wound. And he'd left his shirt and all his gear behind.

Her fingers curled into the fabric of his shirt. Without realizing it, she buried her face in the collar and breathed in his scent.

"Maybe you'd better put that on," he advised.

She jumped, but slipped her arms through the sleeves of the shirt and wrapped it around her. It would get cold tonight. She picked up the *bourque,* but didn't put it on. Instead, she ran her hand through her short crop of curls.

She spent a long afternoon waiting out the sun. With nothing to do except nap and watch the water droplets form on the clear plastic, time passed slowly.

Finally the sun set and Zach said it was time to go. They gathered up their fresh water supply, and packed up camp.

"What are we going to do when we get there?" she asked. "Steal a plane?"

"Yes."

"What if we get caught?"

"That's a chance we have to take."

She sucked in her breath. He looked at her and in a gentler tone said, "We're not going to get caught."

After a couple of hours, a control tower came into view, heavily guarded by men wearing green turbans.

Cloaked by darkness, they kept to the shadows. Zach might not have known where they were going, but he seemed to know what he was doing.

There were no large commercial jetliners at the airport. Only small commuter planes. And a couple of cargo planes. The cargo planes looked to be Russian surplus. If she searched her memory hard enough she could probably even remember the exact make and model from fighter school.

One of the supply planes had its cargo door down and was being unloaded by forklifts. They watched the operation from the shadow of a nearby hangar.

For the next hour they watched the plane being unloaded, circling the hangar at regular intervals as the guards made their rounds.

There was a flurry of activity as the last crates

were put on forklifts. The cargo door of the plane started to close.

"Time to go," Zach said under his breath. "Now," he barked at her when she didn't move fast enough.

He sprinted into the hangar and jumped through the closing cargo door, disappearing inside. She followed, and when she reached the chest-high lip of the cargo door, he pulled her inside just as the door closed completely. Someone shouted from the lighted bay that warehoused the plane's cargo. They'd been spotted.

Instinct moved her toward the cockpit. She plopped down into the right seat. Zach was in the left, their hands met on the throttle in the center. He surrendered control, trusting her to do the job.

She fired up the engines. The heavy cargo plane picked up speed as they taxied down the runway. He pulled back on the stick, taking them airborne.

She'd almost forgotten that butterflies-in-the-stomach feeling of takeoff.

THEY FLEW INTO Turkish airspace without incident until they reached the American military base.

Zach zeroed in on the tower frequency. "Tower, permission to land."

"Identify yourself."

"We're an unarmed Russian-built aircraft carrying precious American cargo."

The air traffic controller hesitated. "Repeat."

"We've recovered Navy pilot Lieutenant Michelle Dann. We're just trying to bring her home, Tower," Zach explained. The tower remained silent. "Permission to land."

"Russian craft, permission denied. Divert to civilian airport."

"Negative, Tower. We're out of fuel."

"Assume holding pattern, Russian craft."

"I'm not kidding."

"Neither am I."

A few minutes later two F-16 Falcons whizzed by. One rolled out to come around behind.

"Looks like we have an escort." Zach tried to offer her a reassuring smile, but he was playing this all by ear himself.

Michelle lowered the landing gear, and they touched down on a runway full of emergency equipment. Then taxied down the runway behind a military jeep as they'd been instructed.

As soon as they came to a complete stop, they were boarded by armed soldiers shouting instructions.

Zach saw Michelle's panic-stricken face. "It's all right," he tried to reassure her in the second before the soldiers entered the cockpit.

"Hands on your head!" the sergeant shouted.

Twenty-four hours later
HOLDING FACILITY,
Incirlik Air Base, Turkey

ZACH LAY on the bare mattress of the rack in his holding cell staring at the ceiling. Well, this was a familiar feeling. His injured arm began throbbing, but he barely noticed.

"Zach?" Michelle called to him from the other cell.

"Right here, sweetheart."

Before she could say more, a commanding voice rang out. "I understand you're holding a couple of my men."

The instant Zach heard Admiral Dann, both feet hit the floor. He moved to the bars just in time to see the airman pop to attention in response to all that gold braid standing opposite his desk.

Michelle stood, equally anxious.

"Sir. Yes, sir." The young man snapped a sharp salute.

The admiral extended the courtesy and returned it with a casual tip of his hand, not bothering to explain that the Navy didn't salute uncovered or indoors.

"At ease. I can see that you do." Taking in the row of cells, he moved around the desk. "Go ahead and release these men.'' The admiral flashed his credentials.

''I'm going to have to clear it with my commanding officer, sir,'' the airman almost swallowed his Adam's apple making the assertion. ''Security breach, sir. He's holding these people for questioning—''

''See these stars!'' The admiral pointed to his shoulder boards. ''Unless he can pull a five-star general or higher out of his ass, I suggest you start unlocking some cell doors right now, Airman O'Sullivan.''

The soldier tripped over his boots to comply.

''Daddy!'' Michelle ran straight into her father's arms.

Zach extended his hand, but instead of shaking it, the admiral pulled Zach to him in a hug. ''Nice job, son.''

''Ah,'' Zach barely stifled the groan.

''You hurt?''

''Just a graze—''

''Let's get you looked at, anyway.'' Admiral Dann turned to the airman. ''Why wasn't this man given medical attention?''

''I...uh...''

They filed out past the stuttering airman, the admiral bringing up the rear.

"Admiral, sir. I need you to sign these release forms—"

"See this designation?" He pointed to the Trident insignia he wore above his ribbons. "Special Warfare, Navy SEALs. We were never here. I suggest you burn those forms, Airman."

"He's going to be in trouble," Zach observed as they left the building.

"Oh, yeah," Admiral Dann agreed. "But save your sympathy for his commanding officer. By the time I get through with the whitewash, young O'Sullivan will look like a hero."

"It's easier to apologize than ask permission?"

"Exactly."

1555 Thursday
ANDREWS AIR FORCE BASE, MD

HER FATHER'S PERSONAL jet taxied to a stop. "There are people out there, a lot of them." Michelle stared out the window of the Learjet, mortified. She focused on flag-waving patriots, shiny band instruments and... "Reporters! Dad!" She turned on her father.

"The president insisted. It's out of my hands." He addressed her with a patience that set her teeth on edge.

Since she couldn't get a reaction out of her father, she turned on Zach. "I'll just bet you love this."

But his own eyes reflected an ever deeper resentment than her own. Or was it disappointment?

"I didn't ask for any of this," she said with more attitude than grace. She plucked at an imaginary thread from the new flight suit she wore. She realized now why it felt more like a prison jumper. After a quick stop at the base hospital in Turkey they'd been in the air. She'd be forced to play puppet a while longer.

Had there ever been a time when she was in control of her life?

"What do you want, Michelle? Can't you see your dad's bending over backward for you." Zach unbuckled and eased himself from his seat, dwarfing the cabin as he stood.

Seeing no rescue, she made her way to the door just as the stairs were being lowered and the red carpet rolled out. She'd expected the Navy band to start with something traditional, such as the national anthem. So the brassy rendition of the old Bananarama song "Venus" caught her off guard.

She stood at the top of the stairs feeling like anything but a goddess. And she'd crashed into the mountaintop.

Her dad placed a guiding hand at the small of

her back. "Smile for the camera. You're America's favorite daughter."

"What about yours?"

"Mine, too."

"I'm your only daughter."

"And I'm so happy to have you home."

Michelle managed to turn her frown upside down and pass it off as a smile. At the moment she raised her hand to wave, the crowd cheered.

She descended the steps on jelly legs, glad for her father's support. Right now she was Miss Apple Pie, female fighter pilot. But how long would that last once they found out she'd become a conscientious objector.

She wanted out of the uniform.

1735 Thursday
PENTAGON-NAVY ANNEX
Washington, D.C.

ZACH AND THE ADMIRAL stood on the window side of the two-way mirror in a small room off the debriefing room. Michelle sat at a table with a crack team of psychiatrists and intelligence officers who specialized in dealing with hostage situations and post-traumatic stress disorder.

She was being more than a little uncooperative. She refused to talk about her ordeal.

There was a speaker into their alcove, but it was turned off. Zach wished the admiral would turn it on—he had the clearance to sit in if he wanted to—but maybe the man was just as afraid as Zach about what he might hear.

The two of them studied Michelle in silence.

She would shake her head. Spit out a few reluctant words. Then go back to avoiding eye contact by staring out the window.

"They need a woman in there," Zach said, cradling his arm, which was in a sling. "Someone she can trust."

"We've sent for Dr. Trahern," the admiral said. "She should be here any minute. How's the arm?"

"Better."

He'd been looked at and released. The sling was to force him to rest his injured arm. And the antibiotics were to stave off infection.

In the other room the senior psychiatrist stood and exited. A second later the door to their cubby opened.

"Judd." The admiral extended his hand to the Captain Moore. "How's it going in there."

"That's what I wanted to speak to you about, Mitch." The man looked pointedly at Zach.

"Go ahead," the admiral said without dismissing Zach.

"Michelle needs friends and family support to

get her through this. We're not making much progress in there. But I'm going to go ahead and release her to your custody so you can take her home.''

"How soon?''

"Today if you'd like. I'm ordering her into the care of Dr. Trahern. Sloan is experienced with post-traumatic stress disorder. She's had great success with EMDR—eye movement desensitization and reprocessing.'' He scribbled something down on a piece of paper and handed it to the admiral. "Prescription for sleeping pills if Michelle needs them. She expressed some paranoia concerning the Norplant. We were able to remove it this morning. But last night she seemed pretty upset about it.''

"Are you talking about some kind of deprogramming?'' Zach's concern overrode his caution.

"Something like that. But nothing as unabashed, I assure you. Michelle can decide for herself after talking to Dr. Trahern.''

"Of course,'' the admiral agreed.

The psychiatrist glanced toward the other room. "It looks like they're wrapping things up in there. Zach, they're probably ready for you now.''

"Me?''

"Standard operating procedure.'' He held open the outer door and Zach went inside.

"Lieutenant Dann, walk us through your escape again," one of the Intel officers requested.

She looked to Zach for strength, then recounted her story for the hundredth time.

"I heard the click of the chambered round. Then the discharge. Ali shot Ihassan, point blank." The whiny little man had fallen to the dirt floor and breathed his last.

A soft gurgle. That was it.

A fraction of a second in real time.

Then everything went quiet and the dead man lay still, his glassy-eyed stare on the ceiling.

She closed her eyes to shut out the image.

"Where were you while all this was taking place?" the Intel officer asked.

"Kneeling on the floor with my hands tied behind my back."

"You didn't shoot Ihassan Mukhtar?"

"How could I? I was unarmed."

"What about Ali Ra'id?" He consulted the sheet of paper in front of him. "Ra'id is also known as Agent Hassan Rakin?"

"I've told you, I didn't kill either of them."

"I see—"

"Lighten up." Zach straightened from where he leaned against the door. "Can't you see she's been through enough? I don't know what you're driving at, but Michelle sure as hell wasn't in on the plot to annihilate the al Mukhtar. Agent McKenna and his cohorts couldn't just kill her out right. They had to make it look like the al Mukhtar were responsible so they could draw the U.S. into the conflict. McKenna knew it was a long shot that the admiral would let his grief override his reason so he threw me into the mix.''

"Sit down, Lieutenant Prince,'' the Intel officer ordered. "We'll get to you. Now, Lieutenant Dann, how did you...escape Agent Rakin?''

"I rolled onto my back and kicked Ali in the stomach, knocking him off his feet.'' If he was going to kill her, too, she sure as hell wasn't going to make it easy for him. At the time she'd had no idea Ali was a CIA agent. No idea McKenna was, for that matter, or that he'd wanted revenge against the tribe he held responsible for his brother's death. She'd been fighting for her life.

"He stood up,'' she continued. "Uttered something I couldn't understand. Then proceeded to gather all the weapons in the room.''

"How many weapons?''

"Were you armed at any time?''

"No. Not then.''

"When did you escape Ali?''

The questions rained down on Michelle. The memories wouldn't go away, but she couldn't seem to find the words.

She'd pushed to her feet, determined to take him down with a head butt this time. Mindless of her plan, Ali had wrestled the rumpled blood chit from Ihassan's hand and waved the bloodstained cloth at her.

She'd stopped dead in her tracks.

That was when it had hit her. He'd killed Ihassan because of her. Or at least that's what she'd thought before she learned about McKenna. She'd never know the truth now.

Ali had proceeded to rummage through the pockets of Ihassan's robe. Found her ring, loaded all the valuables in the room onto his person and ordered her to put on the dead man's robe. He'd given her something to cover her hair and face, then insisted she wear it.

Michelle remembered the small chest-level hole in the black robe. There'd been another larger rip in back where the bullet had exited Ihassan's body.

Neither bound, nor free. She'd followed Ali.

Under cover of a moonless night, they'd stepped over the lifeless body of another man to escape the bombed-out building that had been her last prison. It had been then that Ali had explained the situation in broken English she hadn't even known he spoke.

Against Ali's wishes, and using her as a pawn,

Ihassan had attempted to barter for the release of his deserter brother.

He'd failed.

When news had reached them Sadiq was dead, Ihassan had been furious, wanting to avenge his brother's death by killing her on the spot. But Ali had always been in it for personal gain and couldn't see the point.

Her fate had balanced in the palm of a very greedy man.

On the run, they'd shared a bit of crusty bread and goat cheese in an abandoned bunker south of Al Basrah, Iraq, and argued over the direction of travel.

"Omar, my cousin, is a camel trader. He will meet us here tomorrow," he'd insisted.

Michelle had conceded, to a point, still unwilling to trust the man completely, even though he'd gotten them that far. Her gut told her that the U.S. had allies in Arabia and Kuwait.

Either place was where she'd find sanctuary.

"Devil president grant Ali boon?" he'd asked not for the first time. Pulling the rumpled blood-stained cloth from his pocket, he'd read and reread the blood chit.

Ali had had a hard time believing anyone would reward him for the return of a mere woman. Not that he deserved one penny for the weeks of hell he'd put her through.

"Ali, I'm sure you'll get what you deserve." That comment, like most of what she'd said, had gone right over his head. And she wasn't even sure that had anything to do with the language barrier.

The guy had been several apples short of a bushel. He'd held her captive for weeks without taking a course of action, then shot his partner on impulse when he'd realized there was profit to be gained by helping her.

"I want my ring back."

He'd pretended not to understand her.

"You'll get your reward. But I want that ring. The person who gave it to me…he may be dead. It means a lot to me."

He'd shrugged. "The will of Allah."

"Allah wants me to have my ring back."

That night, Michelle had stayed awake hoping Ali would drift off so she could retrieve her ring. And equally important, arm herself.

No such luck.

When the sun had risen, the steady clang of a shepherd's bell had come from the west. She'd searched the horizon and got her first sight of Omar the camel trader approaching on foot, a herd of camels and goats ambling along behind him.

Ali had motioned for her to cover her face, then

had gone to meet his cousin. With a scowl in his direction she'd complied.

While the two men had exchanged pleasantries, Michelle had kept to the background. Once she had a ride she'd part company with Ali.

Ali had waved the blood chit in the face of his cousin and pointed to the items lined up on the ground. The man had said nothing when Ali offered her survival vest and her boots as trade for two camels and safe passage to Iran.

In his frustration, Ali had turned and paced off a few steps in her direction. "He will not trade!"

"Offer him the ring," Michelle had insisted.

He'd looked at her as if she was a lunatic. Then his expression had changed to one of speculation.

"Don't you even think about it!"

Ali had gone back to Omar, pistol drawn. "You will take us with you, old man."

Then Michelle had felt a surge of sheer desperation. "Ali!"

He hadn't even looked in her direction. So she'd picked up a large rock and marched toward him. "Ali!"

That time he turned. And she'd clipped him in the jaw with the rock. He went out like a light.

Clutching the rock, Michelle had stood over Ali. Then she'd darted a glance at the camel trader and kicked the weapons out of his reach. She hadn't known what the old man would do, but he'd looked nonplussed by the situation.

"Will you trade with me?" she'd asked him. She'd dug her knee into the small of Ali's back. He'd grunted, but hadn't come to. She'd checked his pulse, then ripped the cloth from her head and used it to truss him up before returning her attention to the camel trader. "You can have the automatic weapons." She'd made a sweeping gesture.

He'd shaken his head.

"I have gold." She'd pulled the ring from Ali's pocket. "I need two camels."

He'd nodded. But hadn't taken her ring.

She'd dragged Ali to the nearest camel, and amazingly, the animal had kneeled.

Omar had stood by patiently as Michelle hoisted Ali's body across the animal's back.

After all, she couldn't just leave him. He was a wanted man.

Omar patted another camel on the rump and the beast ambled off. One by one the rest followed. When Ali's camel rocked to its feet and headed off in the same direction, Michelle started to panic.

"No, no!" she'd cried to halt the lumbering beast. She'd turned to Omar for assistance. "I'm not going with you to Iran. I'm going to cross the desert into Saudi Arabia."

He'd nodded in his accepting way, then cut a sturdy camel from the herd and led it over to her.

She'd accepted the reins. "Ali—"

"I will see that my cousin gets to Iran. He would not wish to go to Arabia where there is a Bedouin tribe or two that would just as soon cut off both of his hands as trade with him again."

"Well, that explains a lot." Michelle had been too stunned by the fact that the camel trader had spoken at all to question his perfect English.

"He is a thief. But he is family. You need not worry for my cousin's sake."

Michelle had nodded and turned to look out over the desert. At least she had a ride. And her survival vest.

She could cross into Arabia and approach Kuwait safely from the border. In a matter of days she could be home.

"The Lion Prince of the Desert will help you." Omar had bowed his head, then shuffled his feet after his herd.

But it had all been a ruse.

As Michelle told and retold her story to the officers present, the truth had started to become clear.

Cousin Omar the camel trader, AKA Agent Omar Ferran, had killed Ali. All because of Mc-Kenna's desperate attempt to take back control of a situation that had gotten away from him.

Omar had sent her into the desert to die at the hands of the Bedouin. It hadn't mattered which tribe killed her so long as she died looking like a brain-washed rogue warrior who'd joined the al Mukhtar and brought her father into the fray.

But even that had gone wrong for McKenna.

The al Mukhtar may have sought revenge for the deaths of Sadiq and Ihassan by trying to kill her, but the al Ra'id had sheltered her.

According to her father, Navy SEALs had been dispatched to the area on a peace-keeping mission. And once the two Bedouin tribes learned they'd been manipulated by one man, already dead, there was little doubt they'd settle things in a truce.

CHAPTER TEN

One week later
DANN FAMILY ESTATE,
Middleburg, VA

THE ADMIRAL invited Zach to stay in the guest house. Celebrity-owned horse farms populated the affluent area the Danns called home for generations.

Zach clicked on the TV and plopped down on the couch in the small two-bedroom cottage. Zach's family had been frequent guests here, and he considered it his second home. In younger years their fathers had often been stationed together. He couldn't remember a time when their families weren't living close at hand. Or at least vacationing together.

But there was something a bit uncomfortable about his stay on this occasion. Torn between sticking close to Michelle and getting as far away from her as physically possible, he pretty much kept to himself.

Zach flipped aimlessly through hundreds of digital cable channels.

They still hadn't talked about that long-ago pregnancy. And Michelle was in no condition to talk to him about anything. She burst into tears at the slightest provocation these days. He simply wasn't equipped to handle her outbursts. And his inability to help made him feel inadequate.

But he was determined to be strong for her, to somehow see her through this.

In the interim he'd come to realize a few things about himself. Like why he'd never pushed for a physical relationship after that first time. He'd been afraid of repeating the same mistakes. The tight constraints of the naval academy and then the pilot training that had followed had simply provided an excuse to be close, but not too close.

But after one night of lovemaking in the Arabian Desert, Zach's desire for Michelle was now stronger than ever. Coupled with anger, well, that just wasn't a good combination. He didn't know whether he wanted to kiss her or shake her out of her funk, until she was…what? The cool and composed fighter pilot he once knew. Or the hot and cold woman captivated by the desert.

He could only wish he had the answers.

Somewhere in between she'd find herself again.

He just didn't know where he'd stand once she did. And he only had three more days to find out.

Zach flipped between a romantic comedy that ended in tragedy and the Sports Channel. His ten days of convalescent leave were almost over. He didn't even wear the sling anymore. Once his arm was better he'd be off to BUD/S training, giving it the one hundred and ten percent he'd promised the admiral.

He'd kept the lease on his studio apartment back in California. His car. His plane. Everything he owned was there. But his heart, no matter how bruised, would remain here. For the first time ever their lives were about to diverge.

Being alone he could handle.

Being idle was driving him crazy.

Zach switched off the TV set.

He'd been invited to the main house for dinner that evening and every evening since their arrival. He checked his watch. He'd been putting off his departure time so he wouldn't have to make small talk with his godparents, but even small talk beat the hell out of sitting around. And there was always the chance that Michelle would decide to join them tonight.

Zach headed out the door. A half hour later he sat at the dining-room table with his godparents.

The person he most wanted to see was in her room, supposedly asleep.

"I wish you'd make her come down to dinner, Mitch," Augusta Dann said to her husband.

"I'm not going to make her do anything. She's been through enough already."

Zach sipped from his water glass, listening to the same dinner conversation they'd had for the past seven nights. He'd offer to coax her down to dinner. His godmother would bless him and his godfather would tell him to sit down.

About the only time he spent with Michelle was driving her to and from Bethesda for her appointments with Dr. Trahern, her PTSD counselor.

"How late is the library open?" They all turned at the unexpected sound of Michelle's voice. She wore a sunny yellow sweater set and jeans several sizes too big. She wasn't yet back to her normal weight, but she didn't have that hollow look she'd once had. And all the visible signs of her captivity had healed.

"I suspect it's still open," her father said. "Why?"

"I just want to do some research."

"You could use the computer in my office," the admiral suggested.

"I don't feel like using the computer. I'd rather find what I need in a book."

"I could drive you into town," Zach offered before the opportunity slipped away. He stood, placing his napkin on his full plate.

She declined his offer. "I'd like to drive myself."

Everyone was quiet for a moment, not knowing if Michelle's wish to drive was progress or something else.

"That sounds like a fine idea," her mother said. "Why don't you take Zach with you? I'm sure he'd like to get out after being cooped up in that little guest house all week."

Zach could have kissed the woman.

Michelle seemed annoyed by the idea. But either she really didn't care or she was too polite to come up with an excuse. "Dad, may I borrow the Mercedes?"

"Of course."

They headed out through the kitchen together.

"Look, if you don't want me to come along you can just drop me off at the guest house..." Now, why had he said that? They were both being too polite and careful with each other lately.

Michelle plucked the keys to the sports car from a rack by the kitchen entrance. "You're welcome to come along, Zach. I'm just not sure what kind of company I am these days." She took the steps down to the garage.

She was all the company he needed.

Zach followed her out to the garage where they climbed into the little Mercedes convertible. Michelle started the car and they put the top down.

"What are you looking up at the library?" he asked.

She ignored his lame attempt at conversation for the few seconds it took her to back out of the garage.

"The Koran," she finally answered.

And he wished he hadn't asked. She'd become obsessed with Middle Eastern culture. And Zach still wasn't sure how much of that obsession was due to one man in particular.

They drove into Middleburg in silence. Michelle didn't even turn on the radio and he was reluctant to make any further attempt at conversation.

"You had your hair done."

"What?" She spared him a glance. "Oh, my hair. Well, it was pretty bad before, wasn't it?" The corners of her mouth lifted.

"You should smile more often. Your whole face lights up."

She looked at him then, really looked at him. He just wished he knew what the eyes behind the sunglasses would have revealed. "Thank you for that."

"You're welcome."

"No, I mean it. Part of your charm, Zach, is that you know how to compliment a lady."

"And the other part?"

"That's enough. I wouldn't want you to think that you're more than partly charming," she teased.

He relaxed for the rest of the drive. A teasing smile and the knowledge that she considered him at least partly charming was real progress.

Even before Michelle pulled the car into the town square, they could read the sign in the library window.

Closed on Mondays.

Michelle slumped over the steering wheel in frustration.

"We could still get out and have a look around town," he suggested. "I thought I saw a bookstore a couple blocks back." Before he could so much as open his door, she'd backed out of the parking space, cutting off another driver. The guy leaned on his horn.

"In a hurry?" Zach asked.

"I'm just a little rusty behind the wheel."

"What happened to your car?"

"I think Dad said they put it in storage…" She didn't add *when my plane crashed,* but they both knew that was what she meant.

"Where's your Mustang?" she asked. "I'm surprised you've been without it this long. You love that car."

He'd had his vintage '61 Mustang since high school. He'd restored the car piece by piece. The hood ornament alone had cost him one entire paycheck.

"Still in California. You're not the only one who's driving is a little rusty these days."

He left it at that.

They pulled into a parking garage near the bookstore. "I'll miss you," she said.

Okay, maybe he could push it just a little bit. He turned toward her, putting his arm across her backrest. She opened the door, but stayed in her seat. "Michelle, I'll miss you, too. But it's not goodbye. Not forever."

When she looked as if she'd like to bolt, he grabbed her hand, the left one. The one still wearing his ring. He stroked her fingers with his thumb.

"The first phase of SEAL training lasts six weeks. After that I should get a weekend liberty at least. Maybe we should think about spending that time together. You could meet me in Coronado on the last day of Hell Week. And we could head up North to a bed-and-breakfast in Napa Valley. What do you think? Two rooms, no pressure," he prompted, following her silence.

He congratulated himself on the suggestion, simple yet classy, like Michelle. He'd be tired from a week of sleep deprivation, but it would give him something to look forward to. A reason to keep going during six weeks of grueling training. He sure needed one.

She looked down at their clasped hands, then at his face. "I know you want to talk, Zach. But I need more time." She extracted her hand.

And he was left holding air. Before he could say anything else she was gone.

They walked the block or so to the bookstore entrance. She didn't even make a fuss when he opened the door for her. Once inside, Michelle hung out in the religion and travel sections. And the knot he'd been walking around with all day tightened with the pain of a thousand sit-ups.

Did she miss Asad that much? Or was she just trying hard to understand? She loaded his arms with books. While they were in the travel section, he added one on bed-and-breakfasts to his burden.

"I think I'm done," she said at last.

They moved to the cash register where the bookseller rang up their purchases.

"That'll be $116.11," the woman behind the register said.

Michelle stared at her blankly. "I didn't bring any money. Or my purse. How could I forget something like that?"

Zach pulled out his wallet and selected a credit card, which he handed to the clerk. "There's always an adjustment period after a cruise," he offered the excuse. "You know that."

But this cruise had been like no others. They both knew that. Like him, she was no longer attached to a ship or the Air Wing, but assigned TDY, temporary duty under outpatient medical care. So how did they adjust when they couldn't even talk about it?

He took the bag of books from the clerk. "I'd better drive since you don't have your license."

She stared at him for a moment and he thought she'd protest. "I forgot the keys in the car," she said with stunned disbelief.

Michelle ran for the door and all the way back to the parking garage. Zach did the same, more worried about her reaction than the car. They both breathed a sigh of relief when the Mercedes was right where they'd left it.

She climbed in the passenger side and he handed her the books before closing the door. When he climbed in the driver side he saw that she was frantically digging through the shopping bag.

"What's wrong?"

"What's *wrong* with me! I forgot to have the parking ticket validated."

''Is that all?'' He would have laughed, but she was clearly distraught. ''So what? You forgot.''

''I forget everything these days,'' she said in a voice so small and helpless he just wanted to take her into his arms. And he would have if he didn't think she'd push him away.

Instead, he patted her knee.

She shifted her leg away, then leaned back against the seat with her eyes closed.

Zach pulled out his wallet one more time.

Three days later
DR. TRAHERN'S OFFICE
Bethesda Naval Hospital

THIS WAS Michelle's fifth meeting with Dr. Trahern in ten days. And the woman always started their conversation the same way. ''How are you feeling today, Michelle?''

During the first four visits Michelle's answer had graduated from a hesitant, ''fine, I guess,'' to ''fine.'' This time she answered, ''Zach's leaving today.''

Sloan removed her reading glasses and leaned forward in the overstuffed chair. Michelle sat opposite the psychiatrist with her shoes off, her chin resting on her knees.

''How does that make you feel?''

Michelle picked lint from her khaki uniform pants. "Sad. And please, don't ask me what sad feels like."

"You're getting good at this. That was my next question."

"I know, but I don't want to cry today." They laughed instead, Michelle's nervous energy needing an outlet.

"You can invite him in if you'd like. He's wearing out that year-old copy of *Ladies' Home Journal* in the waiting room."

"No." Michelle shook off the suggestion, but her smile remained. Since Zach was practically all she talked about during her sessions she didn't think it was such a good idea. "I'm going to tell him today."

"Good," Sloan encouraged. "Good for you, I think you should."

Always cold these days, Michelle pulled the standard-issue navy-blue cardigan closer. "I've also been thinking about those EDMR treatments we discussed. I'm not ready to try yet, but soon."

"You're making great strides in a very short time, Michelle. No need to rush. But we could cut your sessions back to twice a week if you like, then maybe once a week. You have my home number for emergencies. Don't hesitate to use it. Have you stocked up on the reading material I suggested?"

"Oh, yes." They chatted away the rest of the hour like two friends. That was probably the thing Michelle appreciated most about Sloan Trahern. The woman didn't make her feel like the total basket case everyone else seemed to think she'd become.

She was getting better. Being able to talk about her ordeal helped.

As the session wound down, Dr. Trahern walked her to the door. "By the way, congratulations on making lieutenant commander."

"Thank you." Just that morning Michelle had added the new rank to her uniform. At one time that was all she'd thought about. Not anymore.

She opened the door to the waiting room. As predicted, Zach had been flipping through the women's magazine. He stood as she came toward him.

"Ready to go?"

"I'd like to stop by the florist in the lobby first—if you don't mind."

"Sure," he agreed. He'd also agreed to wear his uniform when she'd asked him, too. In fact, he was too damn agreeable these days. Just like everyone else around her.

"How'd we get to this point? You a lieutenant junior grade and me a lieutenant commander," she asked.

"You took the high road. And I took the low road." His answer was lighthearted.

But not necessarily true.

They rode the elevator to the lobby, then followed the signs posted on the wall.

"You looking for anything in particular? Roses?" he asked as they wandered through the shop.

"Daisies."

Zach handed her a bunch.

"I want 'em all," she said. "I want to buy out the whole shop."

He looked at her strangely, but loaded up her arms as requested. And when she couldn't hold any more he carried the rest.

"I even brought my purse this time," she teased.

"I don't mind treating."

"Okay, fifty-fifty."

But getting to their money with their hands full was another matter. By the time they finished checking out the register and were gathering their purchases to leave, an older woman, who'd lined up behind them, had become very disgruntled.

"My daughter's gallbladder surgery is going to be over before I get through the line," she muttered under her breath.

Michelle turned to the woman. "I sincerely hope so. And I hope that your daughter is well on her way to recovery by the time you get upstairs. Here—'' she handed the woman a bunch of daisies ''—that's for you and your daughter. I'm sorry you had to wait in line.''

The woman mumbled her thanks to their departing backs.

''What's gotten into you?'' Zach asked when they arrived at the car breathless and laughing.

''Just doing my part to make grumpy old women smile.''

They loaded up her dad's Mercedes with the flowers. ''Next stop…?'' he queried.

She met his gaze over the roof of the car. ''I want you to take me to Sara's grave.''

He instantly sobered. ''Of course.''

En route to Arlington she made him stop at two corner flower stands where she proceeded to buy out their stock of daisies as well.

''How are we going to lug all these flowers to the grave site if we can't get a vehicle pass?'' he asked.

''Not a problem, Lieutenant,'' she answered. ''You're driving an admiral's car.''

''How'd I forget that?''

''Did you think all those sharp salutes were for you, hotshot?''

''Actually, I thought they were for America's Favorite Daughter.''

"Please, don't remind me. I have to get up at 0400 tomorrow so a makeup artist and hairstylist can turn me into something I'm not in time for my appearance on "Good Morning America." A regular media circus is set to follow. My dad held them off for as long as he could, but the president insisted. And it's not even an election year. Do you know the White House has assigned me a publicist and a press agent? I shudder to think of it all."

They'd just pulled into the visitor center of Arlington National Cemetery. Zach turned off the ignition and just sat there staring at her.

"What? Why are you looking at me like that?"

"Because you sound great. You look great. Almost..."

"Almost what? Like my old self? 'Cause I hope not. I kind of like the new me. I wasn't so happy before."

He nodded his understanding, but she wondered if he really got it. She'd changed, and from now on there was no going back. Only forward. "It should be you in front of those cameras, Zach."

"Thanks, but I'll pass. As you know, I've got an appointment tomorrow. Besides, you might just find you're a born politician."

"Yeah, right."

They obtained a pass without delay, then drove Memorial Drive at an appropriately respectful

pace, passing row upon row of headstones that re-
minded them of the price of freedom.

"You okay?" Zach asked, pulling to the curb.

"Yeah, I'm going to be…fine." Okay, she'd
been wrong. There *was* one step backward to take.
"Was it a nice ceremony?"

He nodded. They got out of the car and gathered
up all the daisies. Then Zach led the way to Sara's
grave site.

"Looks like her headstone is up."

"Sara Marie Daniels," Michelle read. The stone
gave the date of her death and the date the body
was laid to rest. Zach kept to the background while
Michelle unwrapped bunches of daisies and piled
them on her RIO's grave. When she was finished,
she sat on the ground, hugging her knees and staring at the headstone. "Did you know Sara was
gay?"

Zach moved closer. "I think everyone on the
ship knew that."

"Well, I didn't. And I was the one bunking with
her." Michelle sighed. "I couldn't tell them everything during the debriefing." She looked up at
Zach and he sat beside her. He'd always been such
a good listener.

"Her back was broken. She couldn't move below the waist. She probably had massive internal
injuries, too, because she was bleeding from her

ears, nose and mouth. She knew she was dying. I could see that she was suffering…she wanted me to pull the trigger, but I couldn't…I just couldn't.''

Michelle's throat burned, but she continued. If she was going to make a new life for herself, she was going to come clean about everything. ''Sara said, 'That's okay, Michelle, because I love you.' I said 'I love you, too.' And she said, 'No, I really love you. Now put the gun in my hand.' And that's when I realized what she wanted. We argued. I made all kinds of promises…. I told her I was going to get her out of there. We both knew that was a lie.''

Michelle stared at the toes of her polished shoes.

''I didn't want to give her the gun. But she couldn't reach it without my help. So I placed her pistol in her hand. Then she confessed something to me. She told me she'd reported to Captain Greene that she'd seen you and me in the shower. She thought if I hated you enough, I'd come to love her just a little bit. Then she told me to be strong because she knew you wouldn't stop looking until you found me.'' She turned to Zach. ''I knew it, too. I know what I said in the desert, but I never really blamed you. And it was unfair of me to say so.''

He touched her face. ''Michelle—''

She stilled his hand and his words. Getting too

sentimental would make what she had to say that much harder.

"Zach, I have a confession, too. I was never pregnant.... *We* were never pregnant."

"What are you saying?"

"I missed a period—probably because I was scared and we were stupid. When I told you I was pregnant, I already knew that I wasn't. Eloping sounded romantic. But you got all responsible and wanted to tell our parents.... I got even more scared. I know I'm rambling, but you're just looking at me. Please, say something. I never realized..."

"Why are you just telling me this now?"

"All my life I've been using you as my safety net. It's time I stood on my own two feet." She twisted his ring off her finger and placed it in his palm. "I'm giving you your wings back, Zach. I've been holding your heart under false pretenses."

0700 Monday
NAVAL SPECIAL WARFARE CENTER,
Coronado, CA

"I'M HERE. Now what?" Zach hooked his aviator sunglasses in the pocket of his bomber jacket and handed his service record to Captain Miller as they descended the steps of SEAL training headquarters.

"Now you sweat." The corner of Miller's mouth twitched. "I'm really going to enjoy whipping your smart ass into shape, Prince."

"Aren't you supposed to be moving on up the line to Commander of Naval Special Warfare or something?" Zach asked.

"Not yet. But you're going to wish I had. Check in next door for uniforms and bunk assignment. And see that building over there?" He gestured with Zach's record toward a shack across the grinder where trainees were beginning to assemble. "That's your first stop. The barber."

Zach picked up his gear and started off in the indicated direction.

"One more thing," Miller called after him.

Zach stopped and turned.

"Get a good look at that ship's bell as you walk by. You're going to ring it sooner or later."

Zach knew all about ringing the bell. Coronado had been his father's last command before retirement. Zach had often tagged along. He'd been about nine when his father explained that only quitters rang out before graduating from SEAL training. Of course, once SEAL training was over, the bell was rung with pride. And his father's unspoken implication was that Zach would ring the bell at his own SEAL graduation.

"Do you have a problem with me, Miller?"

Miller closed the distance, getting right in Zach's face. "I have a problem with the fact that you don't want to be here. You didn't have to take the test. You didn't have to pass the physical. I've got the guys on a two-year waiting list who'd do just about anything to be in your boots right now. So if you want to take that personally, hotshot, by all means do."

"I didn't ask to be singled out for special treatment."

"That's good. Because you're not going to get it from me."

No one would accuse his brother-in-law of playing favorites. And that was okay with him. Zach wasn't in the mood to be coddled.

"Dismissed!" Miller ordered.

If he'd been in uniform, Zach would have snapped a sharp salute. His godfather hadn't done him any favors by getting him into the SEAL program.

And he hadn't done himself any favors by showing up. But he'd made a deal. One he intended to keep. And he knew how much this meant to his own dad.

Besides, if he hadn't accepted the challenge,

what would he be doing right now? Trying to patch things up with Michelle? No, he'd never be able to look at her the same way again. He couldn't just forgive and forget—even if his heart didn't want to let go. She'd given him back his wings and he intended to soar.

Zach eyeballed the bell in passing.

His father's directive about quitters was so ingrained that Zach didn't think he could ring out before graduation if he wanted to. Failure was not an option.

After waiting in line for what seemed like hours, the clippers breezed through Zach's hair in less time than a textbook takeoff from a carrier. He scrubbed his hand over the stubble as he rose from the barber's chair.

Following the haircut, he walked through the issuing of fatigues and rack assignment. Afterward he stowed his gear and changed into the uniform of the day—battle dress and combat boots.

The very last thing he did to settle in was rip his lucky charm—the photo of him and Michelle— in half. He couldn't bear the reminder of happier days. But he'd also carried it for so long he couldn't bear to get rid of it. After a few moments' hesitation he hung both halves in his locker as a different kind of reminder.

Despite his father's expectations, he'd grown up

and gone his own way, never thinking he'd find himself back here where he didn't belong. Even though he'd flown fighters for a living, he'd considered himself a lover.

Now he just considered himself a loner.

But training offered the fresh start he needed. This time, his mission wasn't to find Michelle, but to forget her.

Same day
DR. TRAHERN'S OFFICE,
Bethesda Naval Hospital

THE MORNING'S media circus had been even worse than Michelle had predicted. Her makeup had been applied with a heavy hand and her shorter hairstyle teased to astonishing heights. At the end of her interview on "Good Morning America," America's Favorite Daughter had braved throngs of adoring fans to catch the first flight from New York to D.C.

She went straight from the airport to Sloan's office.

"How are you feeling today, Michelle?"

"Alone."

"How does alone feel?"

"Like I've been torn in two and the best part of me is gone."

1200 Tuesday
NAVAL SPECIAL WARFARE CENTER
Coronado, CA

THEY WERE on their way to noon chow, running in formation along the strip of sandy beach parallel to the highway called Silver Strand.

A carful of babes honked. Another stopped to watch. A couple even showed off a little drive-by skin for encouragement. The Navy SEAL wannabes tried hard to keep their bearing, knowing they'd impress the girls that much more if they did.

Zach had once thrived on that kind of female attention. Somewhere between yesterday and today, he'd grown up.

But right now he had nothing better to do with the rest of his life than run until his sides ached. Physical exertion proved to be the outlet he needed.

Better than booze. Better than babes.

Real aches and pains to replace the ones in his heart he couldn't define. And after weeks of being little more than a couch potato he really suffered. He'd let himself get out of shape. The rest of these guys had at least come prepared. They'd been tested, meeting minimal physical requirements. Zach had met those requirements as part of his an-

nual flight physical, sure. But that had been almost
a year ago.

Another fact he'd discovered firsthand, the maximum age for SEAL training was twenty-nine for
a good reason. The body fell apart at thirty. His
original orders had been cut just before that occasion.

The sun beat down. Sweat poured from his
body. The stitch in his side almost doubled him
over. And his lungs felt ready to burst. But he kept
putting one foot in front of the other, even though
they moved like weighted-lead diving boots as
they came in contact with the shifting resistance of
sand.

Nausea roiled through him, his stomach clench-
ing and unclenching in time to his cadence. When
he couldn't stand it another minute, he dropped out
of formation for the second time that day to step
behind an outcropping of rocks where he could
suffer the dry heaves in private.

This time Miller ordered the other trainees to
halt. "Why don't we show our buddy how much
patience we have? Drop and give me ten. In fact,
we'll just keep doing push-ups until Prince decides
to join us."

The unit let out a collective groan, but dropped
to the sand. When Zach rejoined the formation,
they turned on him. Some mumbled under their

breath. Others told him right to his face what they thought.

"Hey, hotshot," Miller called out from the front of the line. "If you can't run and puke at the same time, you're not Navy SEAL material."

No kidding.

Like a siren calling her sailor home, the bell beckoned in the distance. A dozen or so trainees had rung out the first day. A handful more had quit today.

Zach itched to pull that rope. But with grudging respect for what his sister must have endured, he refused to be the family member who rang out.

Five weeks later
DR. TRAHERN'S OFFICE
Bethesda Naval Hospital

LONLINESS HAD BECOME Michelle's best friend, but she'd learned to embrace it and herself.

Perfection was overrated.

Mistakes were par for the course.

She'd started keeping a journal to express emotions she'd buried for too many years. She'd also used it to record every detail of her ordeal from the moment she was shot down.

Michelle folded her hands over the book in her lap.

"How are you feeling today, Michelle?"

She heaved a heartfelt sigh. "Ready!"

"Well, on that positive note, let's get started." Sloan walked across the room to dim the lights, then returned to her seat across from Michelle.

They'd cut back her sessions to once a week, but she was to start eye movement desensitization and reprocessing today. And they'd be meeting daily for as long as it took, one session or a dozen, although eighty to ninety percent of patients needed only three sessions.

EMDR made time irrelevant, allowing the brain to heal at the rate it took the patient to recount the trauma during rhythmical stimulation of eye movements. Innovative in its simplicity, the therapy had gained widespread acceptance and helped more than a million individuals already.

"Follow my pen with your eyes. Tell me about the day you were shot down. You can begin when you're ready."

"Can I start the summer I turned seventeen?"

"You can begin wherever you like."

CHAPTER ELEVEN

Hell Week
NAVAL SPECIAL WARFARE CENTER,
Coronado, CA

THE FIRST FIVE WEEKS had passed in a blur of physical training. While Zach's body grew stronger, his mind played like a broken record, one song, one refrain...

Michelle.

But it was Hell Week that really tested his endurance. And mental stability.

It had started Sunday night with blowhorns. "Move it! Move it! Move it!" And wouldn't end until rock portage later that afternoon—when they landed rubber rafts on the rocks in front of the Hotel Del Coronado.

They'd slept only four hours the whole week and had just completed their last one-hour rest period—this time in mud trenches. A weathered SEAL senior chief with a leathery tan that made him appear older than his forty-some years began drilling them on weapons assembly.

Under camouflage netting providing partial shade, Zach stood at attention in front of a sawhorse and plywood workbench, trainees on either side of him. Somehow he was supposed to make sense of the parts on the table and assemble his weapon.

Over the past few weeks he'd done it hundreds of times in timed drills. But never after five days of little to no sleep.

His hands were shaking. His knees were knocking.

He itched to swipe the buildup of sweat and grime rolling down his face. When he tried to focus, his gritty eyes felt as if someone had taken sandpaper to them.

And his mind had started playing tricks on him. Hallucinations were part of the sleep-deprived training package. He just wasn't prepared for the wavy blue image, taking on a female form as the sun reflected off the ocean. She waved and called to him in her hauntingly familiar song.

Ring my bell.

"Prince!" the senior chief yelled.

Zach blinked away the muse. The old sea dog stood directly in front of him on the opposite side of the workbench. He tossed a condom onto the tabletop and continued making his way down the line passing out rubbers.

"There's no better protection. For either of your weapons. If you get my drift."

That was a lesson he knew, but hadn't applied twelve years ago. *I was scared. We were stupid.*

Zach went through the robotic motions of putting the German-made Heckler and Koch MP-5 semiautomatic back together. All around him trainees in equally sleep-deprived states attempted to do the same.

Click. Snap. Click.

Each blink of his eye lasted longer than the one before, until he was more or less sleeping on his feet....

Zach pushed aside the shower curtain. Wet and inviting, Michelle greeted him with open arms. He stepped under the steamy spray, his shoulders touching two walls of the small stall as he crowded her into a corner.

"Make love to me, Zach." Michelle smiled up at him as she unzipped his flight suit, sliding it past his shoulders. The jumper rode his hips as he held up his arms and she worked his T-shirt over his head. Neither of them could contort their bodies enough to remove the rest of his clothes, and trying became a lesson in frustration.

Soaked through to the skin, he didn't really care

about removing them or his boots when he had his arms full of the woman he loved, wet and willing. He traced her lush curves. Cupped her full breasts and round bottom.

Her arms went around his neck and he brought his lips to hers. She teased him, never quite letting him capture her mouth. When he tried to hold on, her soap-slick body slipped beneath his arm.

Her inviting laughter tinkled like a bell.

He turned toward her and the small bathroom shape shifted into a long corridor. Michelle backed farther and farther away from him down the hall. She curled her finger and beckoned him to follow.

He tried to move, but his feet felt like lead. At first he was walking, then running in weighted boots. Sweat poured from his body, but he couldn't catch up.

There was a door at the end of the endless corridor and he begged her not to go in. As she turned the knob, her skin turned gray and cold, so cold.

The room was so cold.

He was sweating and freezing at the same time.

Michelle lay down on a gurney. "Why didn't you come for me, Zach? Now it's too late," she accused. *Why, why, why?* The single word echoed in his head.

The gurney rolled through a set of double doors. Michelle's color turned rosy. Another man appeared in the sterile setting. Michelle's flat stomach rounded and grew. She smiled up at the other man. The next thing Zach knew, Michelle was panting and bearing down to deliver a baby.

Not his baby.

A wave splashed Zach full in the face. How had he gotten in the water? He barely recalled the senior chief waiting until the last man hollered, "Clear." "Yahoos, get wet. Weapons above your heads! Move it! Move it! Move it!"

But the dream had been real enough.

Zach barely noticed the burn in his biceps as he held his weapon above his head. He'd make it through Hell Week.

Then what?

1300 Friday
HOTEL DEL CORONADO
Coronado, CA

HOTEL GUESTS GATHERED on the terrace of the famous hotel to watch rock portage—the last exercise of Hell Week.

Zach's parents stood among them.

"Michelle!" Lily Prince waved her over. "You look wonderful. I don't think I've ever seen you in a dress. Not since you were a little girl anyway. Love that floral print. Yellow is definitely your color.'' Mrs. Prince hugged her. Michelle had always felt like a giant next to Zach's petite mother. But if she wanted to feel small all she had to do was look up at Zach's father.

''He's in the lead raft.'' Tad Prince offered her the binoculars.

Michelle brought Zach into focus. He looked wonderful.

Shaved head. Stubble-covered jaw. Smudges under his eyes, his muscles bunching and tightening with his movements. As boat captain, he didn't man an oar. His job was to guide them to shore. She took a deep breath, filling her lungs with crisp California air.

She returned the binoculars to Zach's dad. The boats were coming closer, and Zach's mom began taking pictures with a camera that had a huge telephoto lens.

''Zach will be so happy you could join us for dinner,'' Lily said.

''I'm not staying.''

''But you have to.'' Lily lowered her camera.

''Zach doesn't know I'm here. And I'd really appreciate it if you didn't tell him. I just came to see for myself that he's okay.''

''At least stay until he lands,'' Lily coaxed. ''I still have a whole roll to shoot.''

When Michelle hedged, Tad Prince added his

assurance. "We're just a blur up here. They're sleep deprived and concentrating on the task at hand. He'd better be. Or those waves are going to hurl him into those rocks."

Michelle turned back toward the water. She hadn't realized how dangerous the exercise could be. The first seven-man raft pulled close to shore. Zach hopped out. Followed by the rest of his men.

"His job is to lead," Tad explained.

She could see what a struggle working against the waves was. There were a couple of close calls that caused her to suck in her breath. Before she knew it, though, the trainees were safe on the beach.

He really was okay. And now she could leave.

1900 Friday
MANNY'S DIVE,
Coronado, CA

ZACH LEFT Manny's Dive before the party ever really got rocking. He wasn't in the mood to celebrate with the rest of the guys.

Hell Week was over.

Phase I of SEAL training was almost behind him, but there were two more phases and twenty more weeks to go.

He didn't belong. He wasn't a team player.

He knew it. And they knew it.

But as soon as he stepped outside the SEAL bar, Zach realized he wasn't exactly in the mood for his own company. He'd showered and shaved, even managed a nap that afternoon. All dressed up and no place to go except back to base.

He thought about heading to the Officers' Club at Miramar to hang out with other pilots, but he didn't belong there, either.

He had no gold wings. No wingman. No friends.

That left family. And dinner at the Hotel Del Coronado. He drove with the top down on his Mustang, fiddled with the radio.

"...Khanh Asad al Ra'id..." Zach's hand stilled. "...arrived in the nation's capital today to collect on a blood chit." The newscaster went on to briefly define the term blood chit and explain the role Asad had played in the rescue of fighter pilot Michelle Dann.

Zach switched stations.

He'd been out of touch, but he'd thought the story would have died of natural causes by now. Apparently it was about to be revived. How was he ever going to get that woman out of his head if she became a media darling once again?

Kalilah. Darling. Sweetheart.

Zach pulled up to the hotel entrance and gave his keys to the valet. He'd try his parents' room first. They'd given him the number after rock portage. He hadn't committed to dinner, but his parents liked to dine late to avoid the crowds and he knew they'd wait even longer, if they thought there was a chance he'd show up.

He knocked.

His dad opened the door. "Right on time," he said, adjusting his tie. "Lily, Zach's here."

"Give me a minute," his mother called from the bedroom.

Zach followed his dad into the suite. The TV was on, volume down. Asad flashed across the screen and Zach reached for the remote to turn it up.

"That's been the top story all day," his dad said. "Asad's decided on a boon as he calls it. There's to be a state dinner at the White House in his honor. Michelle's attending. And the press picked up on the scent of romance. Now they're blowing it out of the water with speculation."

"What kind of speculation?" Zach asked, but the camera cutie answered before his dad got the chance. Footage of Michelle's return to the States preceded the reporter's segment-ending question. "Sources say the sheik wants only one boon. Did love bloom in the desert?"

"Turn that off," his mother said.

"It's okay," Zach said. "I'm over her."

"Of course you are," his mother agreed. "Oh, here are the pictures of rock portage." His mother handed him the package. "I had them developed at a one-hour photo place."

"You mean you didn't develop them yourself?"

"My equipment is at home. Thought you might like to see them right away."

"Okay, Mom, I'll bite. What'd I do, fall flat on my face in the sand?" He flipped through the photos, looking closely at each one for his snafu.

Him in a raft.

Him in a raft.

Him out of the raft, waist deep in water.

Him falling flat on his face in the sand.

Woman at the rail…watching him fall flat on his face.

"Michelle was there?"

"We promised not to say anything. Pictures are worth a thousand words though, don't you think?"

"Where is she now?"

His mom shrugged. "We'll understand if you can't make dinner tonight."

"Right. I'm keeping this one." Zach dropped the rest of the pictures and bolted for the door. He stopped at the front desk long enough to ask if they had a guest by the name of Dann. She'd checked out that afternoon.

Zach tipped the valet. But sitting behind the wheel he realized he didn't have a course of action.

Should he crawl back because she'd crooked her

finger? He was the injured party here, and he was still pretty damn mad at her. Besides, she'd made it clear that the engagement was over.

To be fair, she hadn't exactly crooked anything. And he knew she'd ended the engagement because she thought he'd want that once he found out she'd lied to him.

And she *had* lied to him.

But did that really make everything that came before and after a lie, too? Didn't he owe it to himself to find out?

I was scared. We were stupid.

She'd wanted to see him today. But she hadn't wanted him to see her. Did that mean she still cared?

This line of thinking was driving him crazy.... For once he wasn't going to try to second-guess her needs.

He knew what he wanted. Why not go for it?

Why not? Well, he would piss off just about everyone he really cared for.

Of course, everyone who really cared would understand, eventually. Zach pulled away from the hotel with purpose. He knew exactly where he was going and what he'd do when he got there.

Several minutes later Zach pulled into the training facility and parked near headquarters. Floodlights illuminated the grinder. The place they'd drilled day after day. But with most of the guys out partying, the barracks were quiet. The cable of the empty flagpole marked time until morning with a steady clink.

Next to the flagpole was the bell.

The ringing of the bell sliced through the night.

The few trainees and instructors still hanging around came running. Hell Week was over. Who'd quit now?

And why?

2315 Sunday
DANN FAMILY ESTATE,
Middleburg, VA

FORTY-NINE HOURS and three minutes after ringing out of SEAL training, Zach rang the doorbell to the Danns' home. He expected the maid, but the admiral opened the door, wearing a bathrobe and a scowl.

"I drove straight through," Zach offered in an attempt to apologize for the lateness of his arrival. He could have flown, but the road trip had given him time to think about this moment. And he'd decided to get it over with rather than wait until morning.

"I can see that. How many speeding tickets did

you get?'' The admiral's gaze shifted to Zach's loaded car.

"Pulled over once, out West. No ticket," Zach answered sheepishly because the highway patrol officer happened to have been a woman. "Would you mind putting me up at the guest house for a couple of weeks?''

"You're always welcome here, Zach. You know where we keep the key."

"I appreciate it." He brought up the subject he'd been dreading. "I take it Marc called."

"The minute you quit."

"In my defense, sir, I want to say I know you're probably disappointed, but you're wrong if you think I'm a quitter. I've never given up on anything important in my life and I don't intend to start now."

The admiral studied him for a moment. "I'm sure you don't know what I'm thinking, Zach. Breakfast is at 0700. If you sleep in, it's up to you to sweet-talk Consuela into fixing you something to eat."

"Thanks. That won't be necessary."

"'Night, then."

Zach stopped the man from closing the door.

"Just one more thing—"

"Michelle's sleeping, let's keep it that way," the admiral said in anticipation of Zach's next words.

"I'm not going to be bothering Michelle while I'm here." The admiral raised a questioning eyebrow, and Zach asked his original question. "Do you still have the old Curtiss Bi-plane? I'd like to buy it."

"That old thing? Never has run, you know. It came with the property."

"Yes, sir, and I'd still like to buy it. For whatever you think it's worth."

"You drive a hard bargain," the admiral said sarcastically. "I'll tell you what. You let me get back to bed before my wife falls asleep and I'll let you have the damn thing. Now, good night, Zach." The admiral closed the door in his face.

Smiling, Zach backed down the steps. Not exactly the confrontation he'd been expecting. Whaddaya know, the world didn't come to an end just because he'd rung out of SEAL training.

He got back in his car and drove the short distance to the guest house. Running his hand along the door frame, he found the key right where he knew it would be. He grabbed a few essentials from the Mustang and let himself in.

In spite of the week of sleep deprivation and the long drive, he was too hyped up to sleep. He turned on the tube, but couldn't sit still long enough to watch a program. Before an hour had passed he'd unloaded his entire car, fixed himself a sandwich and headed toward the barn.

The huge door was falling off its hinges and it took some effort, but he managed to prop it open. He'd brought along a flashlight because he wasn't sure of the wiring inside the barn.

He tried the switch near the door. Nothing.

It could be something as simple as burned-out bulbs, but he knew where the generator was and decided to try that first. Once he got the juice flowing, he found that only half the bulbs were out. He'd replace those tomorrow. Tonight he had all the light he needed to see his first love.

He circled the 1934 Curtiss Bi-plane. They didn't build them like this anymore. Although, after fifty-some years of neglect, her first blush had faded to a rusty brown. She'd need a lot of work. Probably a new engine. But the structure was basically sound.

All the trouble would be worth it in the long run.

Zach climbed onto the wing and settled down to look around his old haunt. This barn held a lot of good memories. And all the shadows of his past.

The hay was older and scattered, but he knew the exact site where he and Michelle had made love for the first time. He shined his flashlight on the spot...

"There you are. I've been looking all over for you." Michelle sat next to him in the apple grove.

"I thought you were still mad at me." His back was against a tree trunk. After they'd gone their separate ways at the air show, Zach had returned to the Dann property.

"I am, but that's no reason for you to miss the fireworks tonight."

"I can see 'em from here. Maybe I'll even climb the roof of the old barn."

"And get yourself killed."

"I like to live dangerously," he teased. "You sure you're still mad at me?"

"No." She studied her toes poking out the end of her sandals. "You just don't get it, Zach. This is probably our last summer together. We'll go off to separate colleges, get different jobs, marry other people... And it's never going to be like this again."

"You apply wherever you want. And I'll apply to the same colleges." He thought that sounded reasonable.

She threw the blue bear he'd won for her at him and stormed off. He picked up the stuffed animal and followed her winding path through the apple grove.

"What?" he yelled after her. She was so hard to figure out, hot and cold like running water.

She stopped. Hands on hips she glared at him. "What do you want to be when you grow up, Zach?"

"You know." They'd only had that conversation about a hundred times. "A fighter pilot."

"Well, that's what I want to be, too!"

"I know!"

"And where had we planned on going to college?"

"Annapolis. The naval academy."

"I've already been accepted. You haven't even applied. I'll be stuck going to the academy without you. And they don't even let women become fighter pilots. I'll wind up flying some kind of supply plane or something." She sniffled and swiped at her eyes.

"I'll get my application in right away. I promise. My dad's alum, my sister's there, my grades are good enough, it's not going to be a problem."

She stopped sniffling. "Promise?"

"Yeah, we're best buds, right? We're in this together. And if you wind up flying a supply plane, I will, too," he said, glancing up. "Looks like rain—" he started in what was almost immediately an understatement.

A flash downpour started. A crack of lightning flashed. Thunder followed.

"Let's make a run for it." He gestured toward the barn.

"Race ya!" She took the lead, then lost her footing in the mud.

"You okay?" He stopped to help. But she used the moment to get to her feet and knock him over. He caught on quickly to her game. And they ran laughing and sliding downhill toward the barn.

"I won!" Michelle touched the door first.

"Only because I let you," Zach boasted.

He had a streak of mud up to his thigh to match the one on her bottom.

"You did not," she teased, trying to squeeze under the eave and make room for him at the same time. "It doesn't matter anyway. The door's padlocked."

"When'd the admiral do that?"

"A while ago. But maybe there's a window out—"

"Stand back."

"You're going to break down the door?"

"Have you got a better idea?"

"This I have got to see."

She stepped out of his way, brushing at the water running down her face. "Hurry up, I'm getting wet."

"I hate to be the one to inform you, but you look like a drowned rat." He sized up the door.

She sized up him. "You look delicious."

He turned to her. "I take back the rat comment." He voice became a husky rasp of awareness. "You look incredible wet."

"So are you just going to stand there? Or are you going to kiss me again?"

"I'm going to break down the door. *Then* I'm going to kiss you." He gave her a cocky grin. She leaned in and kissed him. Just the lightest touch, but enough to make him forget what he was supposed to be doing. By the time they came up for a breather, they were soaked to the skin and huddled together as one shivering mass.

"Shelly, do you know why I know you're going to be a fighter pilot?" he asked. She shook her head. "'Cause I can't imagine heaven without you."

"Zach, sometimes you say the sweetest things. Now, could you get the door open. I'm freezing."

Breaking in proved to be a challenge. But a couple good lock-high kicks left the door hanging from its battered hinges. "After you."

"This place is in pretty bad shape." Broken glass crunched beneath her feet. There were rotten floorboards, falling rafters, empty crates and bales of smelly hay.

"Look! There's our plane. The Renegade." She walked over to the biplane. "When we were kids we'd sit in here for hours. Remember? I think that's why my dad finally resorted to the lock. This place is so old, he probably thought we'd get hurt playing around in here. You're staring at me," she accused when she noticed he hadn't moved.

"Yeah," he admitted, sticking his hands into his back pockets. Her wet T-shirt clung to her body. The white material had become transparent. He could make out the lacy pattern of her bra and the darker area of her nipples.

She knew what he was doing, but instead of calling him on it, she reached for the hem of her T-shirt and pulled it off.

His hands came out of his pockets, but he remained frozen to the spot by her boldness. She wrung out the T-shirt and hung it on one of the wing cables.

"Do you want to try and dry your T-shirt?" she asked with enough innocence in her voice to have him doubting his previous assumption.

He whipped off his T-shirt and tossed it over the nearest cable, then he closed the gap between them from a few feet to a few inches. But his gaze never strayed from those lacy-cupped breasts.

"Maybe I should take it off to dry." She reached behind her.

"No," he snapped.

She looked stricken. But he didn't want to play

this game. The stakes were too high. And he'd already felt as if he'd lost. He'd be damned if he was going to act out some role as she teased them both out of their clothes.

He brushed his thumb over her lace-covered nipple, then cupped the underside of her full breast. He heard her suck in her breath. An incredible feeling of control came over him, even though he was close to losing his. Shyness was not her natural state.

He bared the pink tip of her nipple by pushing aside the fabric with his thumb. He looked into her eyes. "Only take it off if you want me to touch you."

She backed up a few inches until the wing left no room for her retreat. He started to remove his hand from her breast. Not because he wanted to, but because he knew enough to let the girl set the pace. No meant no, even if you were dying for that first yes.

But she surprised him by pressing his hand to her. The she unhooked her bra, though she didn't drop the lacy undergarment completely.

"You're beautiful, Shelly." He wanted to chase away the uncertainty he saw in her face. He was ready, he was more than ready for this to happen.

"Only because you make me feel that way. I'm not even pretty."

She kissed him. Touched him. And the next thing he knew, she was pushing him across the barn toward the hay, leaving shoes and clothes in their wake. He fell backward into the hay. She landed on top of him, straddling him.

"It's my first time, Zach. Be gentle."

She was ravishing him, yet begging him to be gentle—as if he even knew what that meant. He knew the basics, of course. He'd taken sex ed when he was twelve, and he could remember not being all that interested at the time. Now his body was humming on pure instinct.

"I'll be gentle, if you will."

"Oh, Zach. I love you…"

Zach's eyes were forced open one persistent drip at a time. Rain beat down on the roof. He wasn't surprised to find he'd spent the night in the barn. He had a lot of lost sleep to catch up on, but not today.

Gray light leaked in with the drizzle. It could have been morning or afternoon. At least this time he didn't have to put on damp clothes after spending the night with a warm body.

1000 Sunday
DANN FAMILY ESTATE,
Middleburg, VA

"WHAT DOES he do out there all day and night?" Michelle used her fork to push the eggs around her plate.

"Don't know," her father answered from behind his newspaper.

Brunch was always served at this time, and in good weather like today, out on the patio. Zach knew the routine. But in the two weeks since he'd been back he hadn't taken a single meal with them. In fact, she hadn't even seen him except for the few times she'd hear his Mustang either coming or going and would run to a window to have a look.

"Have you tried inviting him?" she asked. "Maybe he doesn't think he's welcome."

Her father just flipped a corner of the newspaper down and then up again.

"Of course we've invited him." Her mother joined them, leaning in to kiss her father who finally put his paper aside.

"Sí," Consuela added. "I even tried to bring him out with one of my cherry pies."

Michelle stabbed at her eggs. She was feeling irritated because of last night, her second dinner at the White House in as many weeks.

Asad had been there. And while she found him charming, she'd grown tired of the media speculation surrounding their recent public appearances—all of which had been arranged. And since the commitments came to her from up the chain, she felt as if she had no choice but to accept them.

Something Asad did nothing to dissuade.

She'd gone along at first, thinking herself a goodwill ambassador, but now things were getting out of hand. She did not want to sit at the breakfast table and see her own image splashed across the society pages.

Michelle shoved her plate aside. "Consuela, could you show me how to bake a cherry pie?"

MICHELLE DECIDED to walk from the main house to the barn. She'd spent the past two hours in the kitchen boning up on the art of pie making. Consuela had then helped her pack a picnic lunch for two. But the special touches, the delicately folded napkins and the chilled bottle of champagne with flutes from her long-abandoned hope chest were all her own idea.

"I thought you might be hungry." She rehearsed small talk as each step brought her closer to her destination. "You missed breakfast, are you hungry? Consuela baked...*I* baked you this pie."

Just the thought of returning to the scene of the crime—the twelve-year-old crime of passion—made her insides turn to jelly. At seventeen, she'd had the nerve to seduce him; at thirty, she barely had the courage to speak to him.

Standing outside the barn, she took a deep breath. The high-pitched hum of equipment told her he was inside working.

She pushed on the door and discovered it was barred from the inside. "Zach?" She called out to him several times and tried pushing on the barn door again. She circled the barn for another way in—there were plenty of broken windows, but they were all too high.

"Zach!" She tried the door again. This time there was a lull in the noise level. "Zach!"

"Yeah?" he answered, but he didn't come to the door.

"Can you let me in?"

"I'm kind of busy right now."

"I brought you some lunch."

"You can leave it outside." The buzz started up again.

Her jelly insides went still. She set the basket by the door and walked off. After a moment of hesitation she returned for the chilled champagne and one of the flutes. He could keep the folded napkins.

MICHELLE FINISHED half the champagne by the time the grandfather clock in the hall struck midnight. She'd waited until her parents were sound asleep, then soaked in the hot tub with a glass of champagne, telling herself she was entitled to a little self-indulgence. After she'd stumbled up the stairs, she'd indulged in her third glass, one too many for her dizzy head.

In the privacy of her bedroom she'd poured a fourth glass of the bubbly, slipping into a T-shirt and crawling between the sheets before she had the chance to drink it.

Her head had barely hit the pillow when someone knocked on her window. She bolted upright in her canopy bed and looked around the room. Nothing out of the ordinary.

But there it was again—a sound as familiar as this room. Pushing the covers aside, she climbed out of bed and padded across the floor.

Somebody was pelting her window with stones! Throwing open the sash, she ducked just in time.

"Incoming," Zach warned a little too late.

"Zach, what are you doing?" Michelle hissed.

"Sorry 'bout that. I didn't hit you, did I?"

"No, but the gardener is going to chase you down with the hedge trimmers for getting his landscaping stones all over the yard."

"How will he know it's me unless you tell him?" His challenge held a hint of amusement. Standing there staring up at her from the edge of the rose garden, he looked like an adorably rumpled Romeo.

"I'll tell him, all right," she threatened.

"You've never tattled on me before. As a matter of fact, I remember we shared quite a few secrets." His voice turned velvet soft, his challenge as sultry as the hot summer breeze.

She inhaled deeply. "What do you want?"

"I brought your picnic basket." He held it up.

"Leave it, I'll get it in the morning."

"Thing is, I got busy and forgot to eat. Thought maybe you'd like to join me. Seems Consuela packed enough for two."

She looked down at her oversize T-shirt, ran a hand through her mussed hair. "Now? Go away before you wake my parents."

"We're not seventeen anymore, Michelle."

No kidding.

"Get dressed and come down."

"I'm not coming down. I've had a rough day. And I'm a mess."

"I don't care about any of that stuff. I'm coming up. Think this'll still hold me?" he asked, testing the rose trellis beside her window.

"Of course it won't." But it was already too late. He'd started to climb. "Zach!" She reached for her silk robe and put it on over her T-shirt.

"Ouch, dammit. There are a lot more thorns on these roses than there used to be."

"That's because there are a lot more roses." She

gasped as he grabbed those first tenuous hand-
holds, then footholds, and inched his way up the
rickety makeshift ladder.

By the time he reached the windowsill, he'd
ripped his hands to shreds.

She heard a snap, and gasped again as his foot
slipped.

He grabbed on to the ledge and shoved the picnic basket through the window.

"It would serve you right if you fell. You weigh
at least a hundred pounds more than when you
were a kid." But to ensure that he didn't, she
reached out the window and grabbed his belt.

They both turned at the sound of the next window being opened.

"Zach?" her mother queried.

"Yes, ma'am?" He dangled there as casually as
if he were entering through the front door.

"You're both consenting adults now. I think it's
time you stopped sneaking in Michelle's window."

"Mother..." Michelle said, shocked that her
mother had known about Zach's nocturnal visits
all these years without saying a word. Of course,
it wasn't like anything had ever happened in her
bedroom.

Even though he didn't appear to need the help,
Michelle hauled Zach in by the belt and they both
fell to the floor.

"Well, I'm not doing that again." He added, "Maybe" as an afterthought as he sat with his back against the window and smiled at her.

Her jelly insides melted into a puddle. "Look at your hands," she said, searching for a distraction. "All I do is patch you up these days."

"They're fine." He waved her off, taking one of the dove napkins from the top of the basket and wiping his hands.

She leaned against the side of the bed and studied him from the safe distance. "My dad told me you quit the SEAL program." *I wanted to hear it from you.* She left the accusation unsaid. He didn't owe her any explanations.

"I did more than that. I resigned my commission. For the first time in my life I'm a civilian."

"What?" She could barely comprehend the word.

"Quite a shocker, huh?" He started to unpack the basket. "This looks like a picnic for two."

"Consuela must think you need to gain some weight. You are looking rather thin."

"Actually, I've gained weight. You wanna feel?" He flexed his biceps.

"No."

"Come on," he persuaded, taking her hand and placing it on his bulging muscle. "It takes a lot of work to get this definition. I'd like to know some-one appreciates it.''

She heaved a sigh and let her fingers trace the sleeve of his black T-shirt. ''Is that what you do all day in that barn? Work out?''

''Something like that.'' He smiled. ''I'm sorry I blew you off this afternoon. I hadn't realized you'd packed lunch for two. You should have told me. I would have taken a break.''

She pulled her hand back. ''I'm sure I don't know what you're talking about.''

He held up the lone champagne flute. ''I couldn't figure out what this was for. But there's the mate and the bottle.''

Gotcha. He didn't say it. But she reached for the glass she'd poured earlier and offered him the bot-tle to fill his, letting him know he'd won that round by default. ''Cheers.''

''You been up here drinking all night?''

''Something like that.'' She pulled her robe tighter.

''Need some company?''

The simple offer and the way he said it made her eyes sting. ''Yes,'' she said in a small voice. ''It's been a helluva few months.''

''Tell me about it,'' he said, laying out their pic-nic. He offered her an egg salad sandwich.

She shook her head. "I wouldn't trust it after twelve hours."

"I'll take my chances, I'm starved."

"Then go for the PB and J," she suggested.

"Roger that," he said, fishing out the peanut butter and jelly sandwich.

She smiled at his pilot's lingo, obviously so ingrained it had become a part of him. "Do you miss it?"

"Sure, but I'm ready to move on. How about you?"

"I don't miss it at all. That's what scares me. I couldn't get in the cockpit of a fighter again, Zach. And now they want to give me my own command."

"It's what you've always wanted."

"It's not what I've always wanted. It's what I've always thought I should want. There's a difference." She looked into her glass. "You just walked away. I can't imagine being a civilian, but I think I envy you."

"Then get out."

"It's not that simple."

"Sure it is."

"For you. If I walk away, they won't look at me as an individual and say she wanted to do something different with her life. They'll look at my sex and decide all women can't handle it. I don't want to be responsible for that.''

"Then don't be. Listen to yourself. You have options.'' He looked at her over the sandwich. "You still want to fly?''

"I miss the blue sky. And the feeling of freedom. This thing with Asad is getting out of control, too. My life isn't my own anymore. I told them this was the end, but agreed to officiate at an air show tomorrow. Look what they faxed over this morning.'' She handed him a script. "Asad is going to ask for his boon. The vice president gets a cute joke about that not being within his power to grant. And then look at my answer.'' She could barely contain her hysteria. "Yes.''

"There's a simple solution.'' He reached for the pen sitting on top of her journal and wrote *No*. "Unless you want to marry him.''

"Of course I don't. And I've told him that.''

The corners of his mouth lifted.

"Are you laughing at me?''

He shook his head, but he was. "If we were talking about a smart-ass pilot you would have cut him off at the knees. Maybe you're trying to let Asad down too easy. But trust me on this. There is no way to soften the blow.''

"So I'm supposed to stand up in front of thousands of spectators and humiliate him.''

"Basically, yes. Or you can marry the guy."

"You're no help," she teased. Then turned serious. "I've missed you, Zach. I always thought we'd be friends forever. No matter what."

"Is that how you see us in thirty years? Still friends? Like our fathers?"

"The best…the kind of friends who can pick up a conversation in the middle even if they haven't seen each other in years…"

He studied her face for a moment. "Sorry, Shelly, I can't fill that role anymore. I'm leaving tomorrow."

"Just like that?" Her jaw went slack. Her heart hammered her chest. "Will I ever see you again?"

"I'm sure we'll see each other. I just don't want you to go on believing things are going to stay the same. I've changed. You've changed."

She took a swallow of champagne. "Is it because—"

"Of one twelve-year-old lie?"

She nodded.

"I'm not happy about it. But I understand a little more than you might think."

"It started out as the truth. At least I believed I was—"

"I know."

"I didn't know how to stop things once they got started. We were making all those plans. It got so out of control.'' Not unlike her life right now. ''And I really wanted...'' She rubbed the bridge of her nose. ''It felt like I'd lost a baby, like I was losing you, too.''

He squeezed her shoulder. ''You never lost me, Michelle. Never. Had you told me, I might have had the chance to feel some relief. Maybe the same loss you felt, I don't know. Instead, I felt like I wasn't good enough for you. I still loved you, but I was afraid to touch you.''

''We lost all those years because I lied.''

His hand was gentle on her arm. ''One lie wasn't the problem. We never learned to communicate before we had sex. Sure we talked, we even listened. I could look into your eyes and know what you were thinking—''

''And I could finish your sentences,'' she broke in. ''But sometimes I was really afraid of the connection...as if I'd lose myself in you.''

''I did lose myself in you.'' He swept his hand along the side of her face to tangle in her hair. ''Not that I minded all that much. I landed on my feet. I'm happy. And I'm going for what I want.''

''I'm glad, really.'' But she felt a little sad, too, because it didn't include her.

''Think about what you want, Shelly. Now, drink up and I'll tuck you into bed.''

She polished off her champagne and crawled beneath the sheets.

He tucked the covers up to her chin. "I actually have a fantasy that involves a room like this," he teased her about the little-girl decor.

Zach wasn't quite sure if it was the champagne or desire shining in her eyes. He would have liked to take her up on the offer, but he simply kissed her forehead. And after packing up the picnic basket, he left.

The admiral emerged from his bedroom at the same time. Clearing his throat, Michelle's father said, "Couldn't sleep."

"We were just talking," Zach said. "There's cherry pie in the basket."

"Sounds good."

They walked in silence to the kitchen, then started eating.

"I wanted to give you this." Zach pushed an envelope across the kitchen table. "Fair market value for that biplane. Prerestoration condition."

"You didn't have to—"

"My accountant suggested it. I've started my own business. Renegade Air. Air shows. Stunt work. The flexibility suits me."

"That sounds about right." The admiral smiled. "How'd your dad take the news?"

"He was pretty cool about it actually."

"Good to hear."

"I'm leaving tomorrow. Headed out to a paying gig in Hollywood."

"Michelle going with you?"

"I don't know. But I rewrote her script. I appreciate the heads-up."

1300 Monday
AIR SHOW,
Andrews Air Force Base, MD

SHE'D WOKEN UP with a champagne hangover. Her first ever. And the first thing she'd seen was the script for today, the one that ended in Asad's proposal. She'd wanted to pull the covers right over her head. How had she let this get so out of control?

But then she'd picked up the sheet and read the single word Zach had penciled in. *No.*

It really was that simple.

At least she'd thought so until Asad stepped up to the mike and the crowd roared with applause.

"This chit promises great rewards in exchange for helping an American serviceman or in this case, woman." He held up the blood chit to more applause. "Payable to the bearer by the United States government. Mr. Vice President," he continued, "I have decided on my boon." More cheers erupted and Asad had to wait until the noise died down before continuing. "I can think of no greater reward than to have the very fighter pilot who fell to earth, Lieutenant Commander Michelle Dann, for my wife."

The roar was deafening.

Michelle's father squeezed her hand. He'd already told her what he thought of this fiasco, but she was determined to put an end to it once and for all. and the only way to do that was to let her voice be heard.

The vice president had followed Asad to the mike. "Khanh Asad al Ra'id, on behalf of the people of the United States, I would like to thank you and your people." He went into specifics and spoke too long. The crowd grew restless. "As you know, this great country was founded on the principles of freedom. Therefore, I'm afraid I can't answer for Lieutenant Commander Dann. But whatever her answer, know that your service is appreciated." He handed Asad a plaque and the press seized the photo opportunity.

Michelle had to wait several more minutes. She smiled and waved and when she did, the crowd completely lost control. She took several deep breaths and waited for the noise to fade.

But the decibel level escalated as several F/A-18 Hornets flew by, leaving red, white and blue jet streams in their wake. The Blue Angels. They'd been introduced to the crowd during their exhibition flight earlier, so the announcer didn't say anything.

Michelle felt as if she would faint if she couldn't get this mockery over with soon. Then another plane flew overhead. An ancient biplane with a banner that said, Marry Me. The crowd started chanting, "Yes, yes, yes..."

Michelle cleared her throat. The mike squealed. She was about to open her mouth when she noticed that the biplane had started a vertical climb, which she knew would stall out the engine. For once the crowd's attention wasn't on her.

The engine stalled and the biplane fell toward earth in a backward spiral. A hush fell over the crowd.

The announcer's frantic voice broke in. "Ladies and gentlemen, don't try this one at home. You're watching veteran flying ace Zach Prince in a maneuver he invented and perfected." As the announcer's voice faded, Zach did an over-the-top roll-out and the engines roared to life.

He made a low pass over the runway, then came back for a landing. Moments later, he hopped out of the flashy red biplane.

"Ladies and gentlemen, Zach Prince!" Cheers erupted. "This former Navy hotshot has something he wants to ask his wingman." It took the crowd quite a bit longer than Michelle to realize what that meant.

Zach jogged across the field in her direction.

Cameras flashed. Reporters were held back by crowd control. Michelle took one, two steps down from the podium and started at a more sedate pace toward him. When the gathered crowd realized they were going to meet in the middle, they started chanting again, "Yes, yes, yes..."

She threw herself into his arms and the crowd noise faded into the background.

"I love you, Michelle. Marry me."

He pulled out the ring she'd returned to him not that very long ago, and the crowd demanded that he get down on bended knee. He complied. "I thought about getting you a bigger ring. And then I thought about what this one represents. You're my past, present and future, Michelle. My life always circles back to you. I would like to be the best friend and lover who's always there for you. The husband who adores you. And the father of your children." He got to his feet. "Will you do me the honor of being my wingman for life?"

She was crying too hard to stop. And even though they couldn't hear his words, the crowd answered for her, "Yes, yes, yes..."

"Yes," she said. "I'll be your wingman. And your wife."

They strolled from the field toward the grandstand. Zach shook everyone's hand starting with Asad.

"They were all in on it?" she asked when they finally had a moment alone.

"I got the idea when the media turned Asad's visit into such a circus. He was just as uncomfortable with the situation as you, but agreed to play along for old time's sake. Come on." They headed toward the restored biplane.

"I like what you've done to her," she commented.

"Lieutenant Commander Dann!" Two young female officers in uniform approached them on the field. "May we have your autograph? We just started flight school this week."

Michelle offered a few words of encouragement as she signed her name to their programs. They waited for Zach's signature next.

"There goes the next generation of female fliers," he said. "I promise you, the world does not stop revolving just because you change course. Trust me, I know that from firsthand experience. If you stay in the Navy, we'll find a way to make it work. The same goes, if you get out. The important thing is that you make the right decision for the right reasons.''

"I already know what I want."

He raised an eyebrow.

"You're at the top of the list. But do you think I'm going to let you be the only stunt pilot in this family? If I'm going to be your wingman, then I'm going to be your wingman. Or maybe you can be mine.''

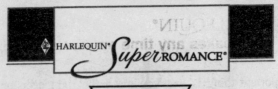

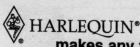

Meet 50 loving dads in

babies
& BACHELORS USA

Take 4 FREE BOOKS,
Plus get a FREE GIFT!

Babies & Bachelors USA is a heartwarming new collection of reissued novels featuring 50 sexy heroes from every state who experience the ups and downs of fatherhood and find time for love all the same. All of the books, hand-picked by our editors, are outstanding romances by some of the world's bestselling authors, including Stella Bagwell, Kristine Rolofson, Judith Arnold and Marie Ferrarella!

Don't delay, order today! Call customer service at
1-800-873-8635.
Or
Clip this page and mail it to The Reader Service:

In U.S.A.
P.O. Box 9049
Buffalo, NY
14269-9049

In CANADA
P.O. Box 616
Fort Erie, Ontario
L2A 5X3

YES! Please send me four FREE BOOKS and FREE GIFT along with the next four novels on a 14-day free home preview. If I like the books and decide to keep them, I'll pay just $15.96* U.S. or $18.00* CAN., and there's no charge for shipping and handling. Otherwise, I'll keep the 4 FREE BOOKS and FREE GIFT and return the rest. If I decide to continue, I'll receive six books each month—two of which are always free—until I've received the entire collection. In other words, if I collect all 50 volumes, I will have paid for 32 and received 18 absolutely free!

267 HCK 4534
467 HCK 4535

Name	(Please Print)		
Address			Apt. #
City		State/Prov.	Zip/Postal Code

* Terms and prices subject to change without notice.
  Sales Tax applicable in N.Y. Canadian residents will be charged applicable provincial taxes
  and GST. All orders are subject to approval.

DIRBAB01R   © 2000 Harlequin Enterprises Limited

*Harlequin truly does
make any time special. . . .
This year we are celebrating
weddings in style!*

A
Walk
Down
the Aisle

WEDDING CELEBRATION

To help us celebrate, we want you to tell us how wearing the Harlequin wedding gown will make your wedding day special. As the grand prize, Harlequin will offer one lucky bride the chance to **"Walk Down the Aisle" in the Harlequin wedding gown!**

There's more...

For her honeymoon, she and her groom will spend five nights at the **Hyatt Regency Maui.** As part of this five-night honeymoon at the hotel renowned for its romantic attractions, the couple will enjoy a candlelit dinner for two in Swan Court, a sunset sail on the hotel's catamaran, and duet spa treatments.

A HYATT RESORT AND SPA

Maui • Molokai • Lanai

To enter, please write, in, 250 words or less, how wearing the Harlequin wedding gown will make your wedding day special. The entry will be judged based on its emotionally compelling nature, its originality and creativity, and its sincerity. This contest is open to Canadian and U.S. residents only and to those who are 18 years of age and older. There is no purchase necessary to enter. Void where prohibited. See further contest rules attached. Please send your entry to:

Walk Down the Aisle Contest

In Canada	In U.S.A.
P.O. Box 637	P.O. Box 9076
Fort Erie, Ontario	3010 Walden Ave.
L2A 5X3	Buffalo, NY 14269-9076

You can also enter by visiting www.eHarlequin.com
Win the Harlequin wedding gown and the vacation of a lifetime!
The deadline for entries is October 1, 2001.

Makes any time special ®

PHWDACONT1

HARLEQUIN WALK DOWN THE AISLE TO MAUI CONTEST 1197
OFFICIAL RULES
NO PURCHASE NECESSARY TO ENTER

1. To enter, follow directions published in the offer to which you are responding. Contest begins April 2, 2001, and ends on October 1, 2001. Method of entry may vary. Mailed entries must be postmarked by October 1, 2001, and received by October 8, 2001.

2. Contest entry may be, at times, presented via the Internet, but will be restricted solely to residents of certain geographic areas that are disclosed on the Web site. To enter via the Internet, if permissible, access the Harlequin Web site (www.eHarlequin.com) and follow the directions displayed online. Online entries must be received by 11:59 p.m. E.S.T. on October 1, 2001.

   In lieu of submitting an entry online, enter by mail by hand-printing (or typing) on an 8½" x 11" plain piece of paper, your name, address (including zip code), Contest number/name and in 250 words or fewer, why winning a Harlequin wedding dress would make your wedding day special. Mail via first-class mail to: Harlequin Walk Down the Aisle Contest 1197, (in the U.S.) P.O. Box 9076, 3010 Walden Avenue, Buffalo, NY 14269-9076, (in Canada) P.O. Box 637, Fort Erie, Ontario L2A 5X3, Canada.

   Limit one entry per person, household address and e-mail address. Online and/or mailed entries received from persons residing in geographic areas in which Internet entry is not permissible will be disqualified.

3. Contests will be judged by a panel of members of the Harlequin editorial, marketing and public relations staff based on the following criteria:

   - Originality and Creativity—50%
   - Emotionally Compelling—25%
   - Sincerity—25%

   In the event of a tie, duplicate prizes will be awarded. Decisions of the judges are final.

4. All entries become the property of Torstar Corp. and will not be returned. No responsibility is assumed for lost, late, illegible, incomplete, inaccurate, nondelivered or misdirected mail or misdirected e-mail, for technical, hardware or software failures of any kind, lost or unavailable network connections, or failed, incomplete, garbled or delayed computer transmission or any human error which may occur in the receipt or processing of the entries in this Contest.

5. Contest open only to residents of the U.S. (except Puerto Rico) and Canada, who are 18 years of age or older, and is void wherever prohibited by law; all applicable laws and regulations apply. Any litigation within the Province of Quebec respecting the conduct or organization of a publicity contest may be submitted to the Régie des alcools, des courses et des jeux for a ruling. Any litigation respecting the awarding of a prize may be submitted to the Régie des alcools, des courses et des jeux for or for the purpose of helping the parties reach a settlement. Employees and immediate family members of Torstar Corp. and D. L. Blair, Inc., their affiliates, subsidiaries and all other agencies, entities and persons connected with the use, marketing or conduct of this Contest are not eligible to enter. Taxes on prizes are the sole responsibility of winners. Acceptance of any prize offered constitutes permission to use winner's name, photograph or other likeness for the purposes of advertising, trade and promotion on behalf of Torstar Corp., its affiliates and subsidiaries without further compensation to the winner, unless prohibited by law.

6. Winners will be determined no later than November 15, 2001, and will be notified by mail. Winners will be required to sign and return an Affidavit of Eligibility form within 15 days after winner notification. Noncompliance within that time period may result in disqualification and an alternative winner may be selected. Winners of trip must execute a Release of Liability prior to ticketing and must possess required travel documents (e.g. passport, photo ID) where applicable. Trip must be completed by November 2002. No substitution of prize permitted by winner. Torstar Corp. and D. L. Blair, Inc., their parents, affiliates, and subsidiaries are not responsible for errors in printing or electronic presentation of Contest, entries and/or game pieces. In the event of printing or other errors which may result in unintended prize values or duplication of prizes, all affected game pieces or entries shall be null and void. If for any reason the Internet portion of the Contest is not capable of running as planned, including infection by computer virus, bugs, tampering, unauthorized intervention, fraud, technical failures, or any other causes beyond the control of Torstar Corp. which corrupt or affect the administration, secrecy, fairness, integrity or proper conduct of the Contest, Torstar Corp. reserves the right, at its sole discretion, to disqualify any individual who tampers with the entry process and to cancel, terminate, modify or suspend the Contest or the Internet portion thereof. In the event of a dispute regarding an online entry, the entry will be deemed submitted by the authorized holder of the e-mail account submitted at the time of entry. Authorized account holder is defined as the natural person who is assigned to an e-mail address by an Internet access provider, online service provider or other organization that is responsible for arranging e-mail address for the domain associated with the submitted e-mail address. **Purchase or acceptance of a product offer does not improve your chances of winning.**

7. Prizes: (1) Grand Prize—A Harlequin wedding dress (approximate retail value: $3,500) and a 5-night/6-day honeymoon trip to Maui, HI, including round-trip air transportation provided by Maui Visitors Bureau from Los Angeles International Airport (winner is responsible for transportation to and from Los Angeles International Airport) and a Harlequin Romance Package, including hotel accomodations (double occupancy) at the Hyatt Regency Maui Resort and Spa, dinner for (2) two at Swan Court, a sunset sail on Kiele V and a spa treatment for the winner (approximate retail value: $4,000); (5) Five runner-up prizes of a $1000 gift certificate to selected retail outlets to be determined by Sponsor (retail value $1000 ea.). Prizes consist of only those items listed as part of the prize. Limit one prize per person. All prizes are valued in U.S. currency.

8. For a list of winners (available after December 17, 2001) send a self-addressed, stamped envelope to: Harlequin Walk Down the Aisle Contest 1197 Winners, P.O. Box 4200 Blair, NE 68009-4200 or you may access the www.eHarlequin.com Web site through January 15, 2002.

Contest sponsored by Torstar Corp., P.O. Box 9042, Buffalo, NY 14269-9042, U.S.A.

PHWDACONT2